SENSORY

DE-TAILS

SENSORY DE-TAILS

Copyright © 2020 by individual authors

Book design by Thurston Howl
Cover art by Thiger © 2020

First edition, 2020. All rights reserved.

A Thurston Howl Publications Book
Published by Thurston Howl Publications
thurstonhowlpublications.com
Fernandina Beach, FL

SENSORY DE-TAILS

EDITED BY THURSTON HOWL

A THURSTON HOWL PUBLICATIONS BOOK

CONTENTS

HEARING

TASTE

Introduction

Thurston Howl

When I started getting into furry fiction, especially in the horror genre, I found myself frequently frustrated with a pattern I noticed in furry writers. In a world where people have animal characteristics, these furry characters wouldn't be able to smell the blood in the room. They wouldn't hear a person breathing behind the trees. They wouldn't see in specific colors. In a nutshell, these furry characters were only furry in appearance. So, I started this book as a challenge to writers: write furry erotica with the core argument of, "[insert sense here] is the sexiest part of furry erotica!" And they rose—in more ways than one—to meet the challenge.

The Sight section showcases Kyell Gold and Weasel. While one features a blind protagonist, the other has an explosion of color. The Smell section includes Joel Kreissman and Shoji. One focuses on artificial pheromones to help with gender transitioning, and the other tackles musk play. Touch has Tarl "Voice" Hoch, Kuroko, and Nathanial "LeCount" Edwards showing off their skills, with elements such as arachnids feeling its prey through web vibrations, an s/m scene with lots of textures, and a touch-by-touch fairytale journey in the woods. The Hearing section features Jay Coates with a story about echolocation and Al Song with a bit more musical sex. Finally, Taste includes Linnea "LiteralGrill" Capps and Patrick D. Lambert. One story tackles the taste of a beaver's anal glands, and the other looks at oral fixation in a sweaty locker room.

Part of what I love about this collection is the immersion. When I look at these stories, I feel my senses activated. And part of that immersion inspired a "deluxe" version of this book. (If you haven't checked it out yet, go to boundtales.storenvy.com to look up the deluxe package.) The deluxe gift box, while much more expensive, includes physical segments to accompany each individual story. The Smell section has accompanying colognes. The Taste section has latte recipes. Touch has physical textures, furs (faux), and fabrics. The Sight section has full-color art prints. And the Hearing section has a CD with accompanying tracks. Again, each element corresponds to a story in that section.

In a nutshell, this project has been such a treat to work on, and the authors have been such joys to work with. I owe all the authors a tremendous thanks, and I hope that you, dear furry reader, enjoy what's ahead yourself.

See the bodies intertwining.

Hear their soft sounds.

Smell the perfumes and colognes.

Taste the wine.

And feel fur against fur.

I think you'll enjoy this…unless my senses deceive me.

Ever onward,
Thurston Howl

SIGHT

Paths

Kyell Gold

(CW: some expression of ableism)

My arms were starting to get tired. "How much longer?" I asked.

Jenny's voice came from somewhere down my right side. "This last swirl is tricky." Her brush tickled my hip fur again, the rich smell of the temporary ink floating in a wave up to my nose.

I sighed and wriggled my fingers. "Can I put my left arm down?"

"Oh. I guess so? Don't smudge anything though."

"How would I tell?" I lowered my left arm carefully to my side, but keeping it an inch away from the fur there wasn't much easier than keeping it straight out.

"That's the point. Just don't brush the fur."

"I thought this stuff dried quickly."

"So did I." The brush on my fur stopped, and Jenny's voice got more exasperated. "But you smudged one of the patterns on your shoulder and it took forever to get out and re-do—"

"I remember. I was here."

"—so just be careful, okay?"

I flicked my ink-free tail. "The whole point of this is for someone to touch it eventually."

"The *whole* point?"

"Enh." I wiggled the fingers of my right paw. "A majority of the reason to walk half-naked around a fantasy convention."

Jenny dabbed at the fur with her brush, tickling lightly, but I have good self-control and I did not twitch. Except for my tail. "All right," she said. Her claws tapped on her phone. "Let me just see here...okay, I need to go a bit higher here."

The brush was already right at the hem of my boxers. "Really?"

"Goes almost to his butt." She set the phone down. "Of course, we could just skip that. I mean, your shorts will probably cover it."

But not, of course, if I wanted to take them off. "Go ahead." As her fingers pushed up the hem of my boxers, I said, "If I'd known he has this many markings, I would've just..."

I didn't have anywhere to go with that, and Jenny knew I didn't, so she just kept brushing the ink into my fur. After a second, I said, "Cren just told me they were sexy markings."

"We're not talking about him," she said firmly.

"I know." Outside in the hotel hallway, a group of people walked by laughing, talking about a friend of theirs who'd gone home with her boyfriend and was going to miss the parties tonight. I listened to them while Jenny's fingers brushed up my hip and I thought about Cren anyway, even though his touch was nothing as gentle as hers.

Then she brushed ink into a stripe coming around the front of my thigh, and my sheath noticed the touch and responded. I bit my lip and tried to think of less sexy things, but the self-control that served me so well when she was tickling me deserted me, and my only hope was that she was kneeling at an angle where she wouldn't notice.

She finished and then gave a short little puff of breath with a "heh," and I knew right away that she'd seen. "Really, Kesh, aren't you supposed to be gay?"

"It's been two weeks!"

She moved around to my other side. "That's all it takes? Lucky Puck doesn't have marks on his sheath. You'd have to do those yourself."

"The brushing is very...it feels good." I couldn't even adjust myself or hide it behind a fold in my pants, or sit down or hold a notebook in front of it. There it was, just pushing out the front of my boxers.

"Yeah, I can tell." Her fingers moved up the hem of the

boxers on that side. "Just think about something unsexy. Anyway, it's not like I've never seen you bulging out before."

My ears flattened. "All right, that was an unsexy enough time."

"What? When you and that red fox, what was his name...?"

"Oh! I was thinking of the beach."

"Oh god, the beach." She laughed. "Yeah, all right."

And fortunately, my erection went down so I was presentable by the time she'd finished. "There. Now your convention hookup will be impressed by your dedication to the role."

"Hopefully by the time he's looking at those markings, he'll be impressed by other things." I swished my tail. "Thanks, Jenny."

"No worries." The smell of ink faded considerably as the screwtop lid scraped closed, and then Jenny's possum scent came up to my nose. "Here, since I saw you..."

She took one of my paws. "Oh, no," I said, "you don't have to this time."

"Fair's fair, and anyway, I kind of like it."

So I let her guide my paw to her breasts and gave them a brief grope each. We'd worked out years ago that since I see with my paws and nose, if Jenny catches a revealing glimpse of me, I get to feel something revealing about her. Jenny's not really interested in guys mashing her tits, or sticking their paws on her tail or whatever, but she says the way I feel is different and interesting, so she's willing to let me do it once in a while. Three times now, over the five years we've been friends.

"Okay, and now I'm changing into those shorts, so you can leave the room unless you want to get groped again."

She pretended to think about it. "You know, I would, but I need to get changed myself. Yell if you need something."

I waited until she'd gathered up her clothes and the bathroom door had clicked before pushing my boxers down and taking them over to the dresser where my bag sat. I put them into the dirty clothes compartment and then felt around in the main compartment for the shorts Cren had bought me and the belt pouch I was going to wear under it with my phone, ID, room key, and so on.

The belt pouch sat snugly against my hip, hopefully not smudging the ink. The shorts were, Cren had told me, patterned to look like a loincloth, with wide stripes of fur down each hip. He'd painted them with the markings that would've shown through if Puck wore a loincloth, and had tried to dye the fur to look the color of my sandy fennec fur rather than the white they'd come in. I had no idea how well he'd succeeded, but I slipped them on and hoped for the best.

When Jenny came out, I caught the strong scents of vinyl and lycra. "C'mere, let me see you," I said, and she walked over to stand in front of me. As I felt the lycra on her arms and the vinyl belt at her waist, she leaned around and rotated my shorts an inch.

"There," she said. "Now they line up pretty well. I did an awesome job."

"I'd expect no less from Vicious Vixen. How does the tail feel?"

"You tell me."

She turned and let me feel the fluffy wrap she'd fastened around her furless pink tail. "Very foxy," I said. "You look amazing."

"You look pretty good, too. Ready to go slay the crowds?"

My cane leaned against the dresser, and beside it, the gnarled wooden walking stick I'd gotten. I wrapped my fingers around the wood and tapped around myself experimentally. Heavier than the cane, more unwieldy, but I navigated by sound and whiskers as much as the cane; the white and red stick served more as a warning to those I was approaching, and I only really used it in crowds, like when we'd gone to the Creators panel.

I planted the walking stick in the carpet and said, "I believe the weather will favor our upcoming journey. Let's set forth."

Once I've done my first walkthrough of a place, I know it pretty well (another thing I sometimes use a cane for; whiskers are good for navigating past moving things, but the cane helps me find furniture). I could've found the elevators without Jenny, but even though she knows I'm pretty self-reliant, she likes to do things for me, so I let her.

Noise and scents burst over me as soon as the doors opened onto the party floor. People shouldered past me into the elevator, and Jenny's paw pulled me out. We stood there in the elevator lobby and absorbed the environment, her with eyes and me with ears.

"Sounds like more parties to the left," I said.

"Oh, but Kesh, you should see this gorgeous cacomistle who just went to the right. She's alone, and she's wearing this sheer green dress."

I squeezed her paw. "Sounds like she might need a superheroine."

"No, no, I'm not going to leave you right away. We have to go to at least one of these parties together."

"No, we don't."

I tried to let go of her paw, but she wouldn't let me. "The flyer for the people who are running CostumeCon in 2015 said their party's in 902, which is...to the left."

"All right. Let's go show off our costumes, then."

Most hotels have Braille numbers on the doors now, but it's easier to have someone lead you to the right door, especially if they also help part the crowd for you. Jenny forged ahead determinedly, and I bumped into a few people, but not so much that anyone commented on it. Scents rushed by me, spandex and cotton and musky fur, deer and a trio of hares and a fox and coyote, and I listened to their conversations, the snatches I could catch.

Mostly they were talking about what kind of booze was in the parties, or arguing about Game of Thrones. One person stopped Jenny so abruptly I almost bumped into her and said, "Hey, Vee-Vee! You better get your own movie soon!"

"You know it!" A slap of paws. "Hey, you look amazing," Jenny said. "Did you sew that yourself?"

While that was happening, a paw landed on my side. Fingers pressed into the bare fur just under my ribs and claws tickled my skin. Predator, then, and big, judging by where the breathing was coming from. I sorted his scent as soon as I caught his breath: wolf. Wolf who had been drinking margaritas. "And who are you, besides the sexiest little fennec in this hotel?"

I straightened. "I'm Puquanah, a shaman of the...Well, I'm not of any tribe right now."

"A shaman, eh?" The fingers slid up and down my side. "So you can...tell my future?"

"Hey." Jenny's voice rang out sharply. "I didn't hear him say you could touch him."

The fingers on my side stilled. "I don't hear him objecting."

"Costumes aren't consent. Kesh—I mean, Puck, come on." The possum's familiar grip closed around my paw. "Sorry, we have to go to a party."

The wolf's paw hesitated just above my loincloth-shorts. "Well, maybe I'll see this cutie later, then."

Jenny knows how to whisper to me. As we walked on down the hall, she asked, "Did you like him?"

"Nah," I muttered back. I couldn't catch his scent around, so I knew he wasn't in hearing range. "He didn't even know who I was."

Of all the conventions I've been to, FanCon has the best parties. There are three kinds of (public) parties: the room party that's the hosts and two of their friends desperately hoping someone else will come in; the party with free booze that's always crowded, drunken, and sticky; and the truly social party where there are some interesting people and it just feels like a fun place to hang out. The parties thrown by convention runners most often fall into that last category, and the party in 902 was no exception.

Jenny and I got drinks, and I sniffed out the food table where there were wrapped chocolates (never take loose candy or chips from a bowl at a party, ugh). We parked ourselves near a couple chairs and talked about her job, both of us also scanning the room for interesting people as we did.

I heard more conversations about movies and books and TV, someone deep into her explanation of an engineering problem she'd solved, someone talking about how long it had taken her to make her costume, a pair of people talking about the other parties on the floor and when they'd leave this one to go back to those, and one person talking about what his vision for the 2015 CostumeCon was. "Anyone look good?" I muttered to Jenny. "No real good conversations."

"There's a cute raccoon over there, but she's with a guy and I think they're together. I can't quite tell, though, they're not talking much."

"Oh, the CostumeCon guy stopped talking. Is he looking at us?"

"I don't know, which one is he?"

"Uh." I parsed the voice in my head. "Tall, deep voice."

"There's a big lion looking our way."

"Might be a lion."

"Now he's walking towards us. And smiling."

We lowered our voices even more. "He's going to tell us about the con," I hissed. "Get a phone call!"

But before Jenny could say anything, a voice boomed out right by us. "Hi! I'm Jory. I'm the treasurer of next year's CostumeCon and I just wanted to say hi and welcome to our party."

"Puck," I said, holding out a paw.

He laughed, so I guess he'd been holding out his paw and I missed it. A moment later he grasped mine and squeezed hard, pumping it up and down. "You're really in character! Awesome! We could use that kind of dedication at CostumeCon."

"I'm Jenny, and we did go this year. It was a lot of fun."

"I wasn't on staff this year, but we're planning all sorts of things to make next year better. Did you see the decorations...?"

He chattered on about his convention and the money they were going to spend on decorations, themed rooms and so on, and I tuned him out, flicking my ears around. More conversations about TV, and then a mild argument that wasn't as hushed as the slightly drunk people probably thought it was.

"I'm going back to the room." Another tall, deep voice, but without the growl of Jory.

"Dude, it's like nine-thirty." Thinner, reedier voice, shorter.

"Exactly. Doesn't Ace Markham come on at ten?"

"You don't come to a convention to watch Ace Markham, dude, you can do that anytime at home."

"They're getting to the glass planet finally."

"And it'll be sitting on your DVR when you get back Sunday night. Look at the people here."

A slight pause, and then Tall-and-Deep said, "I have been."

"The night's barely started! Okay, just one more party, and if you strike out there, I will personally escort you back to the room. You can sit around in your costume and watch TV."

"You said you'd help me figure out which guys might be interested."

"Uh-huh. And what was the first thing I said you had to do?" Tall-and-Deep mumbled something in response. "That's right. And have you even talked to one person?"

"There was that lion who's running the convention."

"Doesn't count. Now look. Anyone here you're interested in? What about him?"

Whatever Tall-and-Deep said in response was lost as Jenny said something that made Jory roar with laughter. I tried to face the voices and hold my drink in a way that showed off my bare chest, but I had no idea if they were even looking at me. I heard Tall-and-Deep say, "Yeah, he's cute," but then Jory was in my face, almost literally.

"And Puck, wait, should I call you Puck? What do you usually do at conventions? How are you liking this one?"

"Puck is fine, or Kesh. I like the creator panels," I said politely. "And just meeting all the great people here."

"Yeah, FanCon's the best. We're hoping to be this big someday." His voice filled my ears and now that I knew he was talking to me, politeness kept me from sweeping my ears to the side. I could barely hear anything else in the room. "But CostumeCon really prides itself on doing things focused toward costumers. Like we have not only a masquerade, but a costume parade. I mean, did you see the masquerade at this con? I guess it's okay, but ours is only a little smaller. Did you go to this one?"

"No," I said, and started to say more, but Jory talked over

me.

"Oh, display not your thing? Well, the other thing we do that FanCon doesn't do is we have a Variety Show Friday night that allows you to do skits. So like, say you had a Ransom to pair with. You guys could put on your own skit."

"I'm not really—"

"Hey, look, that's not for everyone either. I mean, we really want to cater to the fans, the costumers."

Jenny spoke up. "Kesh is, uh..."

"I'm blind," I said. Sometimes you just have to be abrupt.

"I know," Jory said cheerfully. "I read the books."

"I mean, really." I waved a paw in front of my eyes. "Nothin'."

There was a long pause. "Oh. Shit," Jory said.

I braced myself. "It's fine," I started, but he grabbed my arm.

"Are you okay? Can I lead you to the drink table?"

"I have a drink. I'm fine." I tried to wrest my arm away from him.

"Is there anything you need?" He didn't let go, but at least he stopped pulling.

I twisted my arm slightly. "I kinda need you to let go."

"Whoa." His paw released me. "So sorry. Hey, you know, CostumeCon complies with all accessibility laws for handicapped people. We've got wheelchair ramps and...uh. I'm not sure what we have for blind people, but Brian would know." He turned, his loud voice projecting elsewhere in the room for a blessed moment. "Hey! Brian!"

"We're fine," Jenny said.

"Oh, gosh, I'm so sorry." Jory turned back to us. "Look, I'm sure Brian's over there somewhere. I'll just go get him. You guys stay here. But call me! If you need someone to walk you around, or...I'll be right back."

I felt the vacuum left by his departure in more than just the brush of air on my whiskers. "Let's get out of here," Jenny said.

"Yeah..." But I hesitated, listening for Tall-and-Deep again. I didn't hear him or his companion anywhere. "Okay, right behind you."

We hurried out into the hallway, me trusting Jenny to clear a path and not to stop short without warning. She had her paw around mine and she not only pulled me forward but pushed back when she had to slow or stop, so I didn't run into her. "Well, sorry about that," she said. "How about you pick the next party? But at least make it one where there's one other girl."

My ears perked and flicked around, mapping out the hallway and the conversations going on. "No promises. But you can leave whatever party if you don't like it."

"Only if one of us gets lucky." She squeezed my paw.

"I'm lucky even if I don't get a hookup," I said, and she laughed at that. "Now let me listen."

So we walked on slowly. I listened to the parties as we passed them, hoping to catch Tall-and-Deep again, but even though I didn't hear him at the second one, the tone of the conversations sounded upbeat and fun, and I could smell at least three different kinds of alcohol. And there were at least three feminine voices. "Let's try this one," I said, and Jenny guided me in.

"Want a drink?" she asked.

"I'm okay for now." I could feel a wall behind me, and we seemed to be out of the way. "I'll wait here."

"Okay." Jenny's paw gripped my forearm. "I'll be right back."

Then she was gone. I leaned back against the wall and breathed in scents and listened for conversations. I heard at least two people talking about costumes, one complimenting someone else's and another talking about how much time it had taken her to make hers. There was an interesting conversation going on (around a corner, it sounded like from the echoes): a light-voiced guy and a girl talking about their speculation on the future of Castle Destiny, a show I enjoyed because the dialogue was great. I listened to them for a little while, and then I caught the word "fennec," and my ears perked. I was careful not to focus in that direction so if they were looking, they wouldn't see that I was listening.

"Yeah," another voice responded, muffled: facing away from me. "He's cute, I guess."

"You guess," the first voice replied scornfully. Lighter than Tall-and-Deep had been, with a predatory growl and a languid pace that made me think cat of some kind. Tiger, maybe. "He doesn't have tits so you don't give a shit."

"It's more because he has a dick that I don't give a shit," his friend replied. "Look, you want to go for it, go for it."

"You think he'll recognize me?"

"You know, Wex, ask me a few more questions like that, and you might grow a pair of tits yourself. Just get the fuck over there."

"Fuck you."

"I told you, not interested."

With that sparkling exchange, their conversation ended. Maybe-Tiger made his way through the party, but I lost track of him in the muddle of people and movement and talking. Jenny should've been back by now, but I couldn't hear her anywhere. It was nice to know that people thought I was cute; first the wolf in the hall, then Maybe-Tiger, so at least my costume was a success. Or my body, which the costume showed off. That felt good, and not just for the obvious reason.

I swished my tail against the wall, and just then Maybe-Tiger's voice sounded in front of me. "Hi," he said, and he sounded different than he had with his friend, more tentative, younger even. But it was definitely the same voice. Was he getting into character? His scent, now that I knew who he was, was cougar, not tiger. Still big, still feline.

"Good evening," I said, ducking my head slightly to get into Puck's mindset.

"I just saw you across the room," he said. "I'm a soldier, and I don't really know anyone here. It looked like you might be alone like me."

"My name is Puquanah, or Puck for short." I smiled up at his voice. "What's yours?"

He cleared his throat. "I'm Xiller," he said.

So he *had* been getting into character. My nose caught the worked leather he was wearing and the brass fittings as well. "It's a pleasure to meet you, Xiller." I transferred my walking stick to my left paw and extended the right. "What brings you here?"

He grasped it, holding for a moment and then releasing. His grip, strong and confident, reassured me about the person in the costume. "I...I shouldn't say." He had the young, naïve manner down pat. "I'm getting trained..."

Nice adaptation of the story to a convention hookup. "Do you not have a place to stay?"

"Oh," he said, and there was a trace of amusement in his tone, "I do, but..." He hesitated. "Might I ask, are you here by yourself? I, uh, I only ask because I...the shamans I've known have always traveled with a companion."

"I did have a companion, but...he is elsewhere amusing himself in...other ways."

He let out a very light chuckle and then stifled it immediately. "Then might I assume you are free?" I didn't answer right away, and he moderated his tone. "I mean...would you be able to...to show me around the area?"

The decision didn't take long to make. This guy sounded nice, he was really going all in on the cosplay, and he was interested in me. I wasn't sure if this was going to lead to private time, but it seemed to be at least wandering toward that neighborhood, and a big cougar would be just the thing to help me forget Cren.

"I'd be happy to," I said, with as much genuine pleasure as I could put into it. Puck, after all, would absolutely help out a lonely soldier to the extent that it was within his power. And if he were in my situation, well...

"That's a relief." I could feel his smile. "I really don't want to go back to the quarters they assigned me tonight."

"There's just...I mean, I do have a friend, and I should tell her..." Where was Jenny? I turned my head and listened, but I still didn't hear her voice anywhere. I held up a paw to 'Xiller.' "If you'll excuse me a moment, I need to...perform a short ritual..."

"Oh, do you believe in the gods?"

Attempting to be canny, trying to catch me out of character. "That's rather personal," I said, "but since you ask, no, I don't.

But this is a ritual...of communication with people I know."

"Carry on," he said, amused.

I reached into the inside pocket of my shorts and flicked on my phone. The Bluetooth clip in my ear chirped. "Text Jenny," I said.

A double beep told me it was ready for me to dictate. "Someone asked me to show him around. I will find you later."

That should be good enough. The program asked if I wanted to send, and I said, "Yes," and then I listened for 'Xiller's' breathing and turned to him. "Ready to go?"

He offered his arm to lead me around before I'd even asked, and I accepted because I liked holding onto him, which was probably the reason he'd offered in the first place. "What would you like to see?" I asked as he led me out into the hall.

"Oh, I'm new in the palace. What's nice here?"

I pretended to think about it. "The gardens are nice, and of course the main hall is beautiful. The tapestries...so much history..." I couldn't imagine what palace Puck would be in, but I improvised as best I could. "Mostly I see the healer's area, of course. With the war going on, I am kept very busy."

"Do you, ah..." He cleared his throat and guided me around a small group of people talking: raccoons, my nose told me. "Is there anything interesting about your quarters?"

"Mine? Oh, well, I..." I let the hesitation hang there for a moment. Puck was also not too shy about his desires—voicing them directly, maybe, but not about letting those he trusted know. "They are comfortable and adequate, and my window looks out onto the," parking lot, "um, stables."

"They sound lovely."

My heartbeat sped up. This was really happening. I fought to keep from smiling too broadly. "I suppose we may pay them a visit, if you like."

Just then, Jenny texted back, signaled by a chime in my ear and the phone reading her words to me: "So sorry met cute porcupine talking about Queenblade you okay?"

"Do you need to check with your friend?" the cougar rumbled next to my ear.

"Uh," I said, throat dry. "Yes."

So I told the phone to reply that I needed the room, and Jenny shot back a text a moment later that just said, "Go for it!"

We had reached the elevator lobby at that point, and 'Xiller's' paw still rested on my arm. I tapped my walking stick on the ground. "All right. I mean, my quarters aren't anything special, but I'd be happy to show them to you. If you like."

By way of answer, he pulled me to the elevators. "Up or down?"

"Up," I said.

A moment later he helped me into the elevator. "Which, um... floor?"

I held up a paw. "Allow me. The wrong combination of elements could be dangerous. I've had a lot of practice at this."

He laughed and stepped back. I ran my fingers over the numbers, finding and pressing the right one quickly, then stepped back into him.

At our floor, we stepped out into quiet and the scent of a sanitized hallway. I led 'Xiller' down the hall to our room, moving confidently until I knew I was close to our door; my whiskers could feel the slight motion of air from under the door in the still hallway, and I knew where to insert my card key. "I share my quarters," I said, "but the other person...won't be back."

The door closed behind us. A moment later, I heard the heavy clunk of the security lock fall into place. "Just to make sure we're not disturbed," the cougar purred.

"Good idea." I tried to sound casual, but I was too excited, tail flicking back and forth. And then he put his paws on my sides and lowered his muzzle to my nose.

He kissed pretty well, I gotta say. And the warmth of his paws on my sides felt good, too. I reached out to touch him for the first time and found the leather and brass I'd smelled. Following it to its edge, I felt cotton below it, but not the smooth processed cotton of a modern t-shirt. This was rougher, almost linen but not quite the right feel: period clothing. "Nice," I murmured, and then felt the solidity of the muscles under the shirt.

"Thanks." He rubbed strong fingers down either side of my spine. "I've got some catching up to do, though."

The paws disappeared from my side, followed soon by the shuffling noises of someone pulling off leather fake armor and a period cotton shirt. I cocked my head, listening and imagining. When the heavy costume hit the floor, I felt him step forward, and I brought my paws out to meet him.

They met bristly cougar fur and warm muscle. I traced my finger pads along the ridges of muscle and bone, building up his image in my mind: about half a foot taller than me, not the most muscular guy I'd ever gotten to put my paws on, but definitely in the top five (more than Cren, I thought with a little smugness). He had a strong jaw, and he flinched when I touched his whiskers. "Sorry," I said. "Just trying to 'see' you."

"It's okay." He put his paws on my waist and rubbed there, fingers finding the top of my hip bones. Now, in addition to cougar, I could smell his excitement and arousal as well, especially when he shifted his weight and his tail came curling around his legs to brush against mine. So I slid my paws down over his shoulders, down his sides to the pants he was wearing, which were the same rough cotton tied at the front with a cord. He had harder leather bracers on over his thighs, which were fastened with some more complicated arrangement of cords that he attended to when my fingers fumbled over them.

Under all that, it turned out, he wore sheer boxer briefs that felt so nice under my fingers (I love the feel of lycra and lycra-assisted fabrics) that I brought my fingers to the front and up the warm hardness there without even intending to (no, honest). He shivered again and brought one of those strong paws down on my shoulder. "You're the healer," he murmured. "Is there...anything wrong there? I want to be in good health for my mission."

"Yes, you do." I brought my fingers back there and felt the shape. He was erect, all the way out of his sheath, pushing at the fabric of the boxers. "I'll have to do a closer examination."

His legs trembled just a bit. "Go ahead."

So I found the waistband and pulled it down carefully. He helped me slide the boxers to the floor and stepped out of them, then waited. I reached out and found his hips, then slid my fingers to his sheath and up his length, the skin warm and taut against my pads. "You seem in excellent health," I said. "But if you'd like to come over to the bed, I'll give you a more thorough examination."

"Lead on, healer," he said.

I made a mental note of where he'd dropped his clothes and then guided him through the room to my bed. He sat on it and waited.

My own erection was pretty full at that point, so I wiggled out of my shorts and dropped my phone's earpiece on the nightstand before joining him on the bed. "Is this part of the examination?" he murmured.

"Trust me," I said, on all fours as I approached him. "I'm a healer. This may seem unusual, but it's all very necessary."

His fingers brushed my thigh fur, so I was ready when they stroked along my balls and then up my sheath and shaft. "I hope you don't mind if I return the favor."

"Not at all." I found his erection again and brought my paw up and down along it. "I think it's very courteous of you. Most of my charges don't think to offer."

His paw curled around my length. "You do this close an examination for many of your patients?"

"Well," I admitted, "no. Only the very handsome ones on secret missions."

He purred, bringing his muzzle to mine again, and we kissed there on the bed, paws holding each other's warmths. My tail wagged, and the arm that supported most of my weight shivered. As we kissed, he stroked me, and I moaned back into his muzzle.

"Lucky me," he panted as we broke the kiss.

"Me too." I let myself down to my side, close against him.

He curled one strong arm behind me and held my shoulders. "How closely do you need to examine this? Like...with your muzzle? Or, uh..." He trailed off.

"This is fine." I slid my paws along him. "I would need

specialized equipment to examine you...another way...but is this all right with you?"

"Yeah," he said. "I just like being close like this."

Hot body and sweet too? I didn't want to hope that this could be more than just a convention hookup, but this guy was pretty awesome. "Can I ask," I said, starting a regular stroking along his shaft, "how you ended up here by yourself?"

"Maybe..." He panted and pulled me closer. "...after."

I wasn't that close, but then again it usually took me a little while. "All right." I varied my strokes a little and got him to squirm against me. "I think my examination's almost over."

"Uh...huh." He pressed his muzzle into my shoulder.

It actually took me the better part of three more minutes to get him off. I kept thinking he was close, and then his shivers would subside. I tried to find the rhythm again, and the second time I managed it. I could tell when he passed the point of no return, when he got all tense and squeezed me, moaning into my shoulder, and then he shuddered and jerked against me. Warmth hit my fingers, and 'Xiller' squirmed, hips bucking. I didn't have an arm around him, but I pressed close as he held me until he relaxed, breathing hot and deep into my fur.

"Gosh," I said, "I hope I didn't smear your paint."

He laughed and kept me tight in his one arm. "You're fine," he said. "Now it's your turn."

There wasn't much I could do about it even if I wanted to refuse, since he had me in his arm and my shaft in his paw. So I leaned into his shoulder, breathed in the smell of his musk, and lost myself in the sensations of his paw stroking me up and down.

Much like his character, he wasn't very experienced. But once I told him to stroke more firmly, he hit the right spots and then was smart enough to keep doing the same thing over and over. I let the waves wash over me, the delicious novelty of a new scent, a new paw, a new presence dragging the most intimate of moments out of me.

"I take a little while," I said softly as I felt his interest flag. "Sorry."

"It's cool." He nuzzled one ear. "I got nowhere to be."

The climax was all the better for the buildup, growing from a warmth in my groin and spreading out to my feet and the tip of my tail. I gasped and stretched my legs out, my feet against his, one paw on his side while the other clutched the sheets between us. And when I came, I yelped once and bucked into his paw over and over. The smell of my musk mixed with his as I heard his satisfied purr against my ear, and finally I slumped against him, panting noisily.

We lay there for a little while, happy against each other, post-orgasmic glow warming me all over. Cren could go fuck himself, I thought, my paw searching out the cougar's sheath to trail up and down it. His shaft was mostly retracted, but he squirmed and purred as I found his tip. 'Xiller's' paw landed on my ears and made me jump at the unexpected touch, but I settled against him and let him stroke them, the touch adding a pleasant tingle to my contentment. He remained quiet, so I said, "You have the makings...of an excellent healer..."

He laughed. "Once this mission is over...er, perhaps I will consider it." Then he cleared his throat. "Ah, my real name's Seth."

"I'm Kesh. Nice to meet you."

His paw landed on my side. Despite myself, I flinched, then relaxed into the hug. "So," he said, "you come to these cons often?"

"Not really." I kept my voice low, aware of the brush of his whiskers against mine, the short coarseness of his fur. "My friends talked me into it."

Soft feline pawpads stroked down my side to my hip. "You make a really sexy Puck. I don't know the stories that well...only read them once."

"I was going to gain more weight for it, but my...I, uh, decided not to." It felt comfortable lying next to him like this. I imagined Puck with Ransom, Volle with Xiller, as different as those pairings were.

Fingers squeezed my side just above the hip. "I agree with the decision. I mean, pudgy Puck is cute and all, but you're really sexy." His whiskers shifted against me, and I brushed my muzzle up and down.

Then he stopped and tensed slightly. "Hey," he said with a little chuckle, "you're freaking me out a bit with the eyes. It's really good, but we're, like, out of costume now."

Here it was. I pushed my muzzle against his shoulder, hiding my eyes. "Sorry," I mumbled.

"No, you're really good, just...hey, is something wrong?"

"I'm, uh. I'm blind," I pushed out. And then I waited.

He didn't say anything for seven seconds. I counted them. And then he said, "Oh."

"I have been since I was five." I tried not to slip into the dull recitation of a confessional, but it was hard when he wasn't responding. "It's okay. I get around fine, and I have a good job."

"I'm sorry." He spoke distantly past one of my ears, not moderating his voice, so it sounded very loud. "I—it must be really hard."

It was like he hadn't heard me at all. "No, it's fine. I mean, technology's great now. My phone talks to me, and I can browse the Internet by talking to it. My whiskers and nose still work so I get around fine." Dammit, I was repeating myself.

"Cool." His paw lifted from my side and patted it. "Ah, you mind if I clean up in your bathroom?"

I rolled away from him, onto my back. "Sure. Go ahead."

It was nice of him to pretend not to be weirded out by it. A lot of people haven't met an actual blind person, and maybe it was just looking into my eyes that made him feel strange. I've heard that before.

It wasn't so nice of him to try to sneak out once he was done cleaning up. I mean, I'd just got finished telling him that my ears and whiskers worked, so you'd think he would guess that I'd be able to feel him coming out of the bathroom, or hear him put on his clothes and pick up his armor. He probably didn't care that I could hear the door close, because by that time he was gone.

Asshole. I pressed my fingers to my eyes and with my other paw, fumbled for my phone. I clipped the speaker back into my ear and said, "Text Jenny. Where are you?"

It didn't seem fair that my tear ducts still worked when the rest of my eyes didn't. But hey, there you are. I didn't cry much, though, and I was done by the time Jenny's reply came through in my phone's silky voice. "Same party. You?"

The last thing I wanted to do was put on my shorts and go back out there, in case I ran into 'Xiller' again. I imagined him pointing me out to his friends in that party, telling them about the poor blind fox. And then I thought, fuck him. Puck wouldn't sit here feeling sorry for himself—well, okay, yes, he had at first, but Shivah had helped with that. I sure as hell wasn't going to let one asshole cougar keep me here on the bed wallowing in self-pity. So I texted Jenny that I'd be right there, because then I'd made a promise and even if my momentary courage left me, I'd have to follow through.

Fifteen minutes later, clean and clothed again, I took Puck's staff and stepped out into the empty hallway. One elevator ride later, I emerged back on the crowded party floor. It smelled different now, the reek of alcohol thicker, the little pockets of musky arousal stronger as I passed by them. I found what I was pretty sure was the same party Jenny'd been in and stopped just inside the door. The mass of people felt confusing and god, what if 'Xiller' had also come back to this party? I couldn't just look around and find Jenny, and I couldn't pick out her scent in the fug of the fifty people here, not to mention the fifty who'd been here and left their scent behind.

Part of me wanted to be mad at her when she didn't come find me right away, but I recognized the signs of a bad mood coming on and headed it off as best I could. It wasn't Jenny's responsibility to look out for me; if I wanted that, I could've just stayed in the damn room and waited until she got back. So I just leaned back against the wall and tried to relax, as air currents and scents pushed my whiskers back and forth.

And then someone stopped in front of me, someone who disturbed the air a good two feet over my head, or at least way beyond the tips of my ears. A deer—no, elk. That explained the height. I smelled linen and cotton, nothing that was obviously a costume. "Are you, uh, are you okay?"

My ears shot up and my tail frizzed a bit at Tall-and-Deep's voice. "I'm—" I cleared my throat of the squeak lodged in it. "I'm fine."

"Did you lose your Ransom?"

I should've known that dressing as Puck would invite that question, over and over again. "I don't have a Ransom," I snapped. "He's—sorry. I'm sorry. You couldn't know."

"Hey." My left whiskers registered movement toward my shoulder, and I braced myself, but he didn't actually touch me. "No, I mean, I saw you before and you were with a Vicious Vixen..."

"Yeah, she's here somewhere."

"She's right over there. Want me to get her for you?"

"No," I snapped again, and again folded my ears down. "Sorry. I mean, no, it's fine, I can text her. Or she'll come over when she's ready."

There was that awkward silence that comes in conversations when people don't know each other. Sighted people look uncomfortably around the room, so I looked away while keeping my ears perked toward Tall-and-Deep. "Well," he said finally, "do you mind some company while you wait?"

I was about to tell him that he didn't have to, and then I realized that if Jenny was visible from where I was, that he must have already realized that I was really blind. I know, I know, I shouldn't be self-conscious about that, but after Cren and then 'Xiller,' I wasn't feeling too confident, you know? Same as if your boyfriend walked out on you because you were too short or the wrong species or something, and then you jerked off some guy and he walked out on you for the same reason. You'd start to wonder if that's how everyone felt, right?

"Nah," I said. "I mean, I'd be glad—you can wait with me."

He settled around to my right, his bulk warm even though he wasn't touching me. "So," I said, "who are you dressed as?"

He chuckled. "I'm just dressed as me. I'm Deya."

I swiveled my ears to my right. "I'm—Kesh. I'm meant to be Puck, though."

"I know."

I cleared my throat. "I'm not just pretending to be blind."

"I figured that, too."

"I'm just making sure." I took a breath. "I figured it was obvious when I couldn't see Jenny."

"Well, yes." He paused. "Also, one of the shaman lines on your lower stomach is smeared."

"What?" I reached toward the still-damp fur. "Dammit, I thought I was careful."

"I figured you might not have noticed, but then yeah, I figured it out." He sounded hesitant, reluctant to talk about it.

"Thanks for telling me. I guess I'll just...go around looking slovenly for the rest of the evening."

He shifted against the wall. "It doesn't look slovenly. It looks like...uh, it looks like maybe you had a good time earlier."

"Well, looks can be deceiving." I paused and then said, "So people tell me."

He made a startled noise and then laughed, spontaneously and loudly enough to stop conversations around us. I grinned despite myself and some life came back into my tail.

"Sorry," Deya said. "Sorry."

"Don't be. It was meant to be funny."

"All right," he said. "Well then, let's hope the rest of your evening looks up. I mean—gets better."

I shifted my weight a bit, just enough to get close to him. "I think we're on the right path," I said.

These Are the Days of Our Lives

Weasel

It was cold. At least, cold enough to make me not want to leave the comfort of my bed. I mean, when you're enveloped underneath thick blankets and a warm body next to you, why would you want to leave, right? Jim slept effortlessly as the sun peered through the blinds. The room was a mess, but I pushed the thought of cleaning up the moment he rolled into me, nuzzling my chest. Dogs are weird sometimes, but this fluffball of a terrier was mine. I'm not giving him up for the world.

I trailed my hand along the tuft of his head, my thumb slowly massaging his ears. I couldn't tell what time it was, but by how bright the sun was, I figured it was probably around eight. Eight-ish. Somewhere around there. I'm probably one of the few Dobermans out there who is fucking terrible with time. But whatevs.

My eyes lingered along the off-white of his fur meshing with my darkened purple body. I always hated how my body went from deep purple to a belly splotch of light. It was like I was some 60s LSD video, only as a person. But I did love how the softness of his fur, the brown spots on his fingers, all blended on top of me when we lay like this. It's a moment that I rarely want to let go of.

If you were to ask him all of this, he'd probably tell you that I'm crazy and that he doesn't know what I see in him. But I see everything in him. As cheesy as that sounds.

From the night stand, I pull out a small box and flip it open. The sun shines on the dark silver metal; the ruby glistens in the morning light. I rub my thumb across one of the skulls on the side of the ring and read the inscription. *Ultimate.*

He always had to have the final say on everything. Playfully he was always right, which is where "ultimate" came in. Our cute way of finalizing who the fuck was cuter or sexier (newsflash: it ain't fuckin me). So it made sense for me to get that engraved on this.

He took in a deep breath against me as I kissed him on his forehead. I closed the ring box swiftly and put it back in the night stand. His eyes slowly opened, his arm draped over my belly squeezed me, and I squeezed him back. He sleepily muttered an "I love you," before he returned to his early morning slumber.

I looked around the room debating on whether I should get coffee, start breakfast, shower, all the things you're supposed to do as a responsible adult. But when his leg curled over mine, I pushed all of that aside and closed my eyes. Who the fuck could leave this guy?

There was something on my dick. My eyes closed. I could feel the moistness of a mouth sliding along my shaft. Taking in a hefty breath, I opened my eyes and grabbed Jim's head, knowing it was him, and thrusted upward. Playful as this terrier was, he had to know I was going to wake up sooner or later. I held him down at the base of my shaft, his white and brown fur meshing with my torso. If lavender and a vanilla latte were a mix, that would be us, he was the swirl and I the purple whipped cream. I don't know what that says about my hair—green is hard to mix in with coffee—but I like to think it's a sugary topping.

When he started to gag around my shaft I pulled him off and brought him in close, sliding my tongue into his mouth.

"Silo," I heard him say, but cut him off before any more words could escape. My hand smoothed down his body grabbing his cock. My hand stroked him firmly as I pulled away and started sucking his neck.

Jim let out a faint whine, his paw grabbing at my back. "I didn't know you'd be this horny," he said beneath rushed breaths. The words fell off his tongue like notes of an acoustic guitar. Smooth when the right hands were playing him.

"You knew the moment your mouth touched my dick," I teased, pushing him to his back. I lubed my cock with spit and rushed right in. He let out a hot yelp as I grabbed his paws and held them above his head. As my hips thrust, I leaned in and nibbled his ear. I could feel his body melting beneath me as my teeth teased him, playfully scratching at the softness of his ear.

"Fuck!" he exclaimed as I pushed myself deep into his ass. He was tight around me: most mornings he was tight, and my cock couldn't get enough of it. His limber body lay helpless below as the bed shook under us. We created an earthquake on new grounds, the frame motioning violently like waves from a bad storm. Each time it hit the wall, a new wave slammed the beach.

I could see the euphoria in his eyes, lids hanging low as he stared up at me. Moans escaped him. They were even breaks of breath merging with trombone wails. My eyes trailed along his abdomen, admiring the arch of his body. His back pushed his belly up towards me, his cock pulsing as I pushed myself in deeper. Spires of light escaped through the window as the blinds shook. Each ray was a spike against our bodies. One beam landed directly on his chest, as if trying to penetrate, but it was only I who could do that today. In this moment he was mine, our bodies blended together in this act of eroticism.

Before my climax rushed his hole, his cock shot his load onto his belly. Strands of his cum flew up to his chest, making a small trail down to his balls. He was a mess, but he was my mess. I leaned in and licked up the trail, my own climax filling his ass as I licked up the last drop.

Grunting furiously, I let go of his hands and collapsed on top of him, my hard yet fading member still inside. Jim wrapped his arms around me, and I him. "Morning, goober."

He chuckled, his chest bouncing like a basketball being passed to a teammate. "I don't think so. I'm like the least goober? You're just wrong."

I kissed his neck again, nuzzling his chin in the same motion, "I'll take it this time, dork."

We lay there in the moment. We could almost sleep again,

but we both knew we had to get up. "I need coffee." His voice was still in that dreamy state, as if exhaustion and sleepiness were co-existent in this world of bliss.

"I suppose it's time for us to get up." My words were groggy. Drained, yet filled with love because who could not love this guy?

"Hey babe," he started, and I looked up at him. A small spiderweb hanging above us in the window frame. Immediately, I flailed, pulling my cock out of his ass and hopping off the bed. In a fit of laughter he slowly rose to meet me. Even when he laughs he's fuckin' cute.

"Why the fuck are you the way that you are..." I say between frightened breaths. He knelt down and pushed my cock in his mouth then pulled off and looked up at me. In a hot second he screeched, mimicking a fucking meme. "Goddammit," I say walking away to start the coffee. He follows me, laughing maniacally, his voice bouncing between the walls of our hallway.

As the coffee brewed, I turned around and leaned back against the sink. The light hit his body just right, encapsulating all of him as he stretched, his cock still semi-hard. "You okay?" he asked, looking at me as if I'm some weirdo on a plane, and I shook my head.

"Yea, I'm just admiring."

"Oh my god! What is your problem?" he said, walking into the living room. He landed on the couch in one full flop. It was always interesting to watch as he landed. As if his body were a cloud plummeting to softer pastures.

"I can't help that you're the sexiest guy I know, babe. Just have to get over it." He glared at me and rolled his eyes. Grabbing his phone, he opened up twitter, the light illuminating his face. "Hey, babe? Don't forget we have plans tonight."

Confusion took him for a moment. "No we don't. What in gay hell do you mean?"

I smirked and moved closer to him. I rested my balls on his face. "I made plans. Just be home tonight, love. I got something for you."

"What is it?" he asked, grabbing my cock.

"I can't tell you! You'll just have to see tonight, nosy."

"Fiine!" he says defeated. And before I could lean in and kiss his forehead, I see the coffee pot overflowing. Black sludge spills over the floor.

"Fuck!" The word jumped from me as I ran to clean it up. I shut off the coffee maker and started wiping the floor. "Coffee's ready."

He always knows how to dress. It was grey outside, but the brown in his ears almost glowed beneath the snow that was dancing around us. Skinny jeans wrapped his legs, curving perfectly around his ass. His tank hugged his belly underneath his jacket. He wore this purple scarf tight around his neck. I always loved when he wore that one. But what can I say, I'm a tad biased. If he wore green or purple I'd melt at the sight of it. I pulled him close to me and whispered in his ear, "What kind of underwear are you wearing?"

He leaned in and kissed my neck and whispered back, "Who says I'm wearing any? And what are we doing at this graveyard?"

"You don't remember this place?" I said coyly, pushing us beyond the gates.

"No, I remember. You're normally not this adventurous though," the boy slapped back quick. I lowered my hand into his jeans grabbing his ass.

"I figured returning to the scene of the crime wouldn't be a bad idea." I led us far into the cemetery. The trees loomed over us, covering any view of the sky we had. At first glance, this place looked haunted, but it does hold a lot of dead people so I guess that's appropriate.

We rounded a bend on the trail. There wasn't anyone around, at least no cars in the area. We were perfectly alone, even though I could feel eyes watching us like the first time we were here. I walked us off the trail, a tree in the corner of this exclusive haunted forest. "Remember when you blew me here?"

"Was it this spot?" he responded, unsure. His eyes darted around looking at the others surrounding us. "I guess this would be it; most look the same," he said with a chuckle.

"Well I'm ready for another round," I said playfully, taking off my jacket and shirt.

He smiled. "You won't be too cold?"

"I think I can keep us both warm." I pushed him against the tree and kissed him hard. My hands pulled his scarf off his neck and draped it above the limb. Next I pulled his hands above his head and tied him there. He shivered when the chill air lashed his ass when I stripped his pants off his body.

"Gonna fuck me hard, daddy?" he asked teasingly. I rolled my eyes and nibbled his ear.

"Of fucking course." I took out my cell phone and snapped a quick picture of us, my cock going hard into his ass. His moans echoed in the air as I grabbed his hips. I grabbed at the tuft of hair on his head and yanked it back, his moans getting louder.

The area around us seemed almost illuminated now. Pants tight around my knees I thrust forcefully against him, and the moment I blinked they were all around us. Spirits. Ghosts. I don't care what you call them. They were around us, watching, yet we didn't care. I moved in and kissed his neck, grabbing his cock quickly. I stroked him hard as I fucked him. Grunted, "I love you," in his ear, and he moaned the words in return.

The world around me seemed to spin. Spirits and grass spiraled as my climax neared its peak. His beige fur flew with the small wind blowing through. I was the purple lighting between us and the dead. Striking the same area several times before shooting my load. My lavender body drained itself of all erotic energy, yet my hands still worked his thick shaft.

"Don't pull out," he practically shouted. Though I was spent, I continued to fuck him. My cock pushing against his prostate. "Fuck yes," he exclaimed, his cock shooting his cum against the tree. Even after he came, I stayed inside him a few moments more before the cold got too freezing for our bodies.

And like that, our audience had gone. I don't know where they went, or if they were even there. But it didn't matter. Ghosts only appear when they want to. That's always been my experience with the past. It's gone. Staying frozen in time, yet when it wants to make itself known, it'll appear. It always does.

I guess they felt the need to come alive. Or maybe we resurrected them.

The glow still remained, this odd sense of energy surrounding us. I snapped another pic or two of his used ass, cum dripping out tastefully. And it was tasty, I would know. I let his arms down from the tree, and we started walking away.

"Wait," I said, and I nudged him forward to the tree again. "There's something inside it. Go take a look." I moved my head towards it. The ring nestled firmly in my jacket pocket. My green hair almost blended well with the dying leaves surrounding us. As if only part of me would be invisible with this half-way complete camouflage. Looking around, it felt as if the trees were slowly glowing around us. The brown leaves and green, frozen grass emanating an energy unseen by many here. For a moment, I thought I saw shadows, greyed bodies standing around, but when I blinked they were gone.

Jim put his hand in the hole and grabbed a slim piece of notebook paper. His feet slowly walked up to me as he read it aloud.

i know it's only been a year

and we've only joined
together for a few months

i ain't the easiest
person to live with

but eros

who could not see the world
inside your eyes

what embers glow beneath your fur
while you sleep, or when you kiss me

you've spoiled me
lover

lured me home
a place i never knew

we are a cocktail
of eroticism
our liquor
blended with
love

so i have
to ask
would you
do me the
honor of
marrying me?

As he read that last line, I knelt on the ground, ring in hand, waiting for his answer.

[Editor's note: I said yes.]

SMELL

Violets

Joel Kreissman

My partner held up the small vial, gazing down her snowy vulpine muzzle at the label. "Synthetic Anthropomorphic Pheromone, *Vulpes alopex*, female." I set a comforting black-furred paw on her shoulder. "That's it then?" I asked. "Your new scent?"

The arctic fox nodded. "My therapist wants me to try wearing it, in public, as Lucy, for the next week before we can progress further. She thinks smelling like a vixen might help me feel more comfortable as one. Depending on how I feel after that we can talk about hormone replacement then."

I nuzzled into Lucas's—no, Lucy's—scruff affectionately, picking up a bit of musk. Lucy used a special shampoo that stripped off most of the testosterone-laden scent, but it didn't get all of it. We foxes are very scent-oriented, like our larger canine cousins, when in sniffing distance of my mate I had to admit it was a bit difficult to think of her as a vixen.

Maybe that was why Lucy was so reluctant to go out in public as a vixen. She would dress up in the house; the first time I'd stumbled upon her trying on a bra we had a long conversation about her feelings, and I told her that I wanted her to be happy. But the one time I had gone out with Lucy in public, she left a trail of sweaty pawprints and panted nervously every time a stranger looked at us.

"Lu…" I trailed off as I thought. "How about you use the pheromones tonight, just the two of us?"

She seemed to calm down a little. "Yeah, just like when I

crossdress with you. No different except you'll smell a vixen too, not just see one."

"Tod, vixen. You are what you are, no matter what you look or smell like." I licked her lightly on the ear. "Now go on, put your perfume on, get dressed. I'll order dinner."

Lucy nodded, requested the Italian place on the west side, and ducked into the bathroom. I ordered a large thing of chicken alfredo and picked out a wine bottle while waiting for it to arrive. I'd just set out plates and drinking bowls when I heard my mate call out, "Tom, can you come help me with this?"

I ran over to the bathroom and as soon as I cracked the door open my nostrils were hit with a pungent musk. Like rotten eggs undercut with violets and a touch of vanilla. Honestly, it wasn't that different from my own musk, but I'd grown used to Lucy's subdued scent, to be hit with a smell that strong so abruptly caught me off guard. The naked vixen was sitting on the lid of the toilet, legs crossed nervously, with an arm draped over her breasts. The scene reminded me of some softcore yiff I'd seen, only I knew she wasn't concealing the same sort of exaggerated attributes those models had. She stared straight at me with big yellow pleading eyes. "Do I seem like a vixen now?" She asked.

Automatically I started to tell her that it was what was on the inside that mattered. But I realized that wasn't what she wanted to hear now. Instead I said, "If I did not know you, I would think you were a vixen."

Lucy's ears turned back against the sides of her skull. "But you know better, don't you?"

"No!" I exclaimed. "Well, yes, I know that your gender is something that you have to figure out yourself. But I don't expect strangers on the street will address you as a tod."

She tensed slightly at the mention of strangers, but nodded. "Yes, yes, thank you." Lucy stood then, slowly drawing her arm away from her flat chest and uncrossing her legs. "There were a couple more glands I wanted you to help me cover. I've already done my paws and cheeks, but not...." Her tail twitched anxiously.

"The caudal gland?" I suggested. She nodded. The big gland

on the upper surface of the tail might be a little hard to reach, yes, but given it was the only one that smelled like violets I was surprised Lucy hadn't applied it yet. "Okay, tell me what to do."

Lucy turned and held her tail up to my reach. "There's a blacklight under the sink if you need to find it. I use it when scrubbing it off."

I found the UV light and switched it on. Her white fur glowed faintly under the ultraviolet, but there was a small patch one-third down the length of her tail that glowed slightly brighter. Curious, I turned the light towards her hands, and they glowed like the wall at a nightclub. Her cheeks displayed fluorescent tear tracks. She blinked as the strayed a bit too high. "It's only the caudal secretions that are supposed to fluoresce."

I turned the light on my own hand, no glow. I grabbed my tail and found a glowing streak running down the orange fur. "I think they mixed them all together."

She held my tail up to her muzzle and inhaled. "You smell different, a bit of old wood in there."

"Well, I am a tod," I replied, picking up the small bottle I found Lucy's violet gland again and prepared to pour the vanilla-like mixture on it. "How much do I put on?" I asked.

"Three drops." The snow fox replied.

My hand trembled minutely as I let the first drop slip out onto the colorless fur. It hung there, a slowly spreading damp patch, as I let the second fall.

"One more…" I said to myself as I tipped the bottle slowly, only for my hand to jolt a quarter of the bottle onto her tail when the doorbell rang.

I froze, the heavy aroma of artificial pheromone evaporating all around me. When the door rang a second time my brain sluggishly formed the connection. "That's probably the delivery guy." I thought out loud as I gingerly set the bottle down. "Sorry. I should go get that."

Lucy nodded. "I'll try to clean this up."

I ran for the front door just as it rang a third time. Outside stood an impatient-looking deer carrying a paper bag with the restaurant logo on it. "Chicken alfredo?" he inquired with a bored tone, just before his nose started to wrinkle in disgust.

"Sorry," I started to explain as I reached for the bag. "We had a bit of an accident while cleaning."

The stag gingerly held the bag of pasta out at arm's length. "You smell like a skunk. What kind of accident?"

I carefully reached for the underside of the bag, briefly touching his hooves as I did so. He flinched at the contact and almost sent the heavy bag tumbling to the floor. Just barely catching it in time. "I don't think you want to know."

"Right, you paid online, right?" I nodded, and the delivery stag turned to leave. Walking off a little quickly, I thought.

I set the bag of pasta on the counter and gave my hands a sniff. Almost immediately I recoiled at the stench of musk and violets, I must have spilled some of the pheromone on myself. By the time Lucy emerged from the bathroom I was on my third soap wash.

She was wearing a bright red blouse that stood out against her white fur over a stuffed bra. Her waist was covered by a knee-length grey skirt that fluttered as her tail wagged. Her face fell almost imperceptibly when she saw me frantically washing my hands. "Did you spill that much on yourself?"

I shook my hands dry and shook my head side to side. "It was my fault, really. I'll try to be steadier next time."

"Next time…" Lucy trailed off in thought. She picked up the bottle of wine I'd picked out and read the label. "Rosé, really? You want a rich white with chicken alfredo."

"Oh." She was more knowledgeable of wine varieties than me, I'd honestly just guessed. "Good thing I hadn't opened that one yet. Why don't you come and pick one out?"

Lucy pulled the tinfoil-wrapped garlic bread and the plastic container of pasta out of the bag and set them on the table. I caught a whiff of garlic and butter as she peeled back the foil and sniffed the bread. Followed by a more subdued scent of chicken covered with melted parmesan. As I watched Lucy gently wafted the scent of the alfredo with one hand towards her waiting nostrils. She inhaled the scent deeply and let it out with a sigh. "Yes, definitely a white." She strode over towards the counter with the liquor cabinet, passing within a foot of me.

I got a fresh whiff of her new scent as she reached past me for the one bottle of white wine we had. The strong aroma of eggs and violets saturated my nostrils again, and I couldn't even smell the wine when Lucy punctured the seal with a claw and held it out for me to sniff. The pungency reminded me of something, but what? The familiarity of the scent dogged at me as I followed my mate to the table with our dinner.

I spooned out pasta and chicken onto our plates as Lucy poured wine into our wide-mouthed glasses. It was a good pairing, from what I could tell, but I barely noticed the taste as I lapped up the wine in between bites. Lucy's scent was just too strong, it kept trying to draw my attention away from the meal, so I kept focusing all the harder on it.

Lucy seemed to notice when I was halfway through my plate, and she had barely started. "Do I really smell that bad?" she inquired.

I snorted into my glass in surprise. "Well, no, I wouldn't say bad," I tried to explain. "More that it's… distracting."

Lucy looked at me skeptically. "What do you mean by 'distracting'?"

"Well," I tried to explain it. "Something about the musk reminds me of something. But I can't for the life of me remember what?"

"Huh," Lucy thought. "You said you've only dated tods before. Were there any situations where you might have been exposed to a large concentration of vixen pheromones in the past? Relatives or something?"

I shrugged. "All I can think of was the first time my sister went into…" It dawned on me, once a year Dad took me and my siblings to a motel for a week and left Mom alone in the house. Then one year I caught a strong smell coming out of my big sister's room, and she started staying with Mom that year. "…heat."

"Heat?" Lucy's jaw dropped. "I smell like I'm in heat?"

"I… suppose." I regretted that pathetic response from the moment it left my mouth. "It's just what your scent reminds me of most."

She gingerly set down her fork and took a long lap of her wine. Staring at me with those black-ringed blue eyes. Lucy took another lap, followed by a deep breath, and only then did she speak again. "Does that... turn you on?"

I dropped my fork in shock, my wine glass started rocking dangerously on its stem before I grabbed it. "What makes you say that?" I asked nervously.

"That's what tods are supposed to want, isn't it?" She answered in a tone that sent chills running down my spine to the tip of my tail. "A vixen ready to be filled with kits?"

"Well, I..." I stammered like a kit at recess. "You know I'm not exactly straight, right?"

Lucy leaned forwards, propping her head up on her arms, a smile slowly emerging on her face. "No, that much was apparent from your string of ex-boyfriends. But, you like vixens too, don't you? I've seen your porn stash."

My ears folded back, and I felt my face flush. Where had this sudden confidence come from? "Yes, I'm bisexual. But that doesn't mean I would go nuts for a vixen in season."

"That's not quite what I said," Lucy responded. "I believe I said 'want'. And I'm pretty sure that is exactly what you want right now." She stood up and strode towards my side of the table. "Do you mind if I come over and check?"

I flinched at that, withdrawing into myself defensively. Though, come to think of it, my pants did feel a little tighter than normal. For some reason I was terrified of what she might find. Curiosity, and a desire to check for myself first, drove me to unzip and take a look just before she started to reach under the table.

As the denim flaps parted and peeled away from my groin I caught a wave of rank sweat-laden musk wafting off my crotch and spotted the first hints of pink flesh peeping out from the end of my sheath. Shocked, I tried in vain to cover it and ended up looking straight into Lucy's brilliant blue eyes. She gave me another foxy smile. "There's no reason to be embarrassed, Tom. It's just me."

Of course, we'd been together for a couple years now, back when Lucy still went by "Lucas." Before he—she—worked up the courage to talk to a therapist about what she'd been feeling. But, something about her seemed different now; part of it may have been the pheromones. Certainly she smelled different, but she was also acting different, more confident and assertive.

When she grabbed at my protruding tip, I decided that I was overthinking it. My mate was in the mood now, and did the reason why really matter? It wasn't anything we wouldn't normally do and we could always figure it out later. I started pulling my pants down to give Lucy easier access.

Lucy reached down to cup my white-furred balls as they were exposed. I reached around her back and felt the straps holding her padded bra under her blouse, I started fingering the clasps before reconsidering. Instead my hand wandered to the base of her tail and started squeezing her cheeks.

I felt Lucy's tail wag, the thick fluff brushing against the sparser fur covering my hand. The polar-adapted fur of her hand tickled the sensitive skin of my cock, prompting a quick snort. She loved doing that. Meanwhile my own hand bunched up her skirt to run my fingers through the fuzz covering her buttocks. I noted quickly that she was not wearing underwear as my fingers probed into her crack. A slight feeling of wetness gave me pause, prompting me to slowly withdraw my hand and cautiously sniff it. The skunky aroma of violets tickled my nostrils again.

Lucy noticed my look of surprise and commented simply, "Anal glands."

That gave me pause. Fingering and rimjobs were a regular feature of our nights together, but I had grown used to Lucy's lack of scent. Comparisons to our feral cousins aside, I was unsure about sticking my nose in such a strong musk.

My thoughts were again interrupted by the unmistakable feeling of Lucy's tongue rasping against my glans. Figuring dinner was done for, I shoved my plate and glass quickly off to the side so she could lean on the table without sitting in alfredo. Following my lead, Lucy plopped down on the table and lay on her side, head and shoulders dangling over the edge to reach into my lap.

I spread my mate's buttcheeks apart as her tongue wrapped around my shaft. She let out a deep-throated purr as my fingers penetrated her passage, dulled clawtips snagging gently on her inner walls. Her muzzle enveloped my shaft, carefully keeping her teeth from penetrating the sensitive flesh. With her lips applying suction my erection swelled to a foot-long rod in seconds.

I could not justify my hesitation any longer. Putting my apprehensions aside I thrust my head between Lucy's legs and under her tail. My chin briefly brushed against her fuzzy scrotum as my muzzle probed for her vixen-scented ring. My nostrils filled with the violet musk as I let my tongue flick out and test the puckered sphincter. I felt her moans climb up my shaft and I responded with a deeper lick, passing through the tight ring.

She cupped my balls in one hand, bracing herself as she swallowed my swelling cock with the other. I pushed my muzzle in so deep it seemed like my cold black nose was actually entering her sweet-smelling anus.

Abruptly my attention was yanked to my mate making a gagging sound. I pulled myself out of her ass to see what was the matter. In Lucy's shocked jaws, at the base of my enlarged shaft, was an angry red bulb the size of a tennis ball. Her teeth started to dig uncomfortably into my swelling cock, I had to get it out of her mouth before she accidentally drew blood. Not sure what else to do I wrenched her head off of mine, wincing as her canine teeth scraped my sensitive skin.

Lucy coughed a couple more times, bringing up a thick phlegm that might have been partially pre-cum. Once her airways were clear she looked down at my swelling in curiosity. "Is that a knot?" she asked, intrigued.

I considered, it looked somewhat like the textbook photos and porn I'd seen before, but there's a massive difference between an image on a screen and something actually attached to your own body.

"It looks like one," I replied awkwardly. "But I've never been with someone during mating season before." Some canine guys like to claim they can get a knot any time, but I figured that was just bravado. I've personally never gone so far as to form a knot.

"It isn't breeding season now," Lucy pointed out.

"That's not what my nose says." I picked up Lucy's pheromone-laden tail for emphasis.

The arctic fox pulled her tail back. "I smell like that from the artificial pheromones. It's not real, I'm not, I can't...." She was struggling to form a new sentence.

I did what I could think of: I laid an arm across her shoulder and pulled her close. "Real enough for me. Pheromones or not, you're my vixen." I glanced down and noticed my knot beginning to shrink. "We might as well not waste that."

Lucy looked down at the organ that had caused her to gag not a minute ago. She seemed to consider whether it would fit in her rear. "I admit," she mentioned. "That I've fantasized on occasion about something like this."

I motioned for Lucy to turn over onto her front. "If it helps," I added, "imagine that it's snowing outside."

Her tail lifted, pulling the back of her skirt up and exposing her buttocks to my view. "Be gentle," she requested, flicking her tail towards my face and sending more violets in my direction. I felt my cock swell again in my hands as I guided it between doughy cheeks and into an already loosened and lubricated pucker. Lucy let out a nervous breath as my tip entered the sphincter and brushed her tail against my muzzle again.

The reinforcement of vixen scent prompted me to push in deeper, bringing the edge of my still exhibited knot up to the ring. Her anus resisted the entry of the bulbous end, bigger than what the orifice normally accommodated. But with one more thrust the muscles yielded, and my knot was free to continue its expansion inside my mate. I rocked back, testing the resistance of the knot inside and saw the skin of her rear draw back with the knot. I thrust forward and felt Lucy purr in pleasure when I impacted her prostate. As I humped her over and over, my knot restricted my movement more, and each thrust became shallower.

Lucy was encouraging me the whole time, whispering things

like "Yes, breed me, please." And I tried to accommodate her by thrusting more powerfully, hot fluids gathering at the end of my cock.

"Come on, Tom!" Lucy suddenly grabbed the front of my shirt and dragged me down on top of her. "Fill me with kits already!"

I wriggled my arms under her waist, pulling her into me as I slammed us into the table with nearly enough force to knock it over. Finally I felt a hot rope of semen burst from my shaft into her bowels. A primal scream erupted from both our throats in unison as we climaxed.

Our wine glasses tipped over, bouncing off the hardwood of the table, spilling alcohol as they rolled. For a tense moment I thought they might roll off, and then I heard a cracking sound from the table legs. I yanked Lucy off the table, my cock still buried in her ass. We stood there, connected at the waist, semen dripping down the front of her skirt, acrid-smelling wine dripping off the edge of the table.

I realized then that my cock was still pumping seed into Lucy, my knot lodged firmly in her sphincter. She started to pull off, only to be held by my knot. "Are we tied?" she asked.

I bent over, trying to spot the cock buried in her. "It seems so." I started to motion us towards the bedroom, figuring that we couldn't do much else until the knot shrank. "Are you convinced you really are a vixen yet?"

She didn't say anything, just wagged her rotten-egg- and violet-scented tail.

My knot took half an hour to shrink enough for us to uncouple and clean up the spills. By then we were too exhausted from the night's activities to do much more than sleep.

I woke up the next morning to the sound of the shower running. Briefly, I wondered who it could be as I could still smell Lucy in bed with me. But, as I reached for her I found her absent from the bed, her new scent had saturated the sheets.

With a sigh, I started stripping off the sheets, but after dropping them in the hamper to be washed I still smelled that cloying odor following me around. I scraped my cheek with one hand and sensed a wave of musk filtering towards my nose. With a snort I ran into the bathroom to try and wash the pheromones off.

I caught sight of Lucy's silhouette through the shower curtain, so I turned on the sink instead and started splashing soap and water all over my face in an attempt to get the musk off. It continued to overpower the astringent soap scent no matter how hard I scrubbed. I was considering reaching into the shower for Lucy's shampoo when a white-furred arm snagged a towel. A minute later a vixen with matted fur stepped out, towel wrapped around her torso.

She spotted me washing my face frantically. Before she could ask, I explained, "Your perfume keeps clinging to my nostrils."

"Oh, pity," Lucy replied. "I was hoping we could go out today and wanted to ask you if I still smelled like I was in heat."

Filthy Coyote

Shoji

I made my way down to Alejandro's apartment a couple minutes earlier than he'd asked me, even though he was fifteen minutes late as always. Approaching his doorway, I tried over and over again to convince myself that this was just a normal, everyday meeting with my landlord. I'd be able to just talk it over with him and be done with it. Truth be told, I didn't know why I even wanted to go through with it. James was the one who was so goddamn sure I would get the gig I just barely looked at, and I sure as hell didn't see him putting in any more time or effort at work. Especially after getting rid of Paul when we needed the money from a roommate, James should be the one here doing this to keep a roof over our heads.

I leaned back against the sunbaked stucco wall, groaning and putting my head in my paws. A look down at my phone said it was already a quarter past three. Maybe Alejandro forgot. Maybe I could just go on a walk to Super 11 and call mom for some help on the way back. Maybe I could drive out to Sangra and meet Norman when he got out of work and just forget about this for a little while over dinner.

I shook my head and stood up straight when I heard a truck pull into one of the spots in front of the complex. I could smell the scruffy coyote before I saw him. He didn't have any of the heavy yet tasteful cologne he usually bathed himself in. Alejandro smelled of earth, crushed leaves, chainsaw oil and most of all, he reeked of sweat and a full day of working out in the sun. He cleared his throat after he ambled up the stairs and swiveled his pointy ears towards me. "'Ey, Remmy, I know I'm late. Tráffico coming up the 5 was chit."

Even though I didn't usually have the best sense of smell, what Alejandro gave off was enough for me to wrinkle my nose and press my ears back. "No worries about traffic, but hey, man, a shower might be nice before we, uh... get down to business."

I looked over him as he got to the top of the stairs and lunged past me to unlock his door. He had a red bandana tied around his ears that made him look less like my landlord and more like a mix of Rosie the Riveter and Tupac Sakur. His always-clean polo shirt was replaced by a faded graphic tee that was covered in spots of drool from panting in the heat. "I was down in frogtown helping out my abuelita with her garden. You're just ganna have to deal with it." He pulled his shirt off and started to unhook his belt, but he paused and looked at me.

I held up one of my webbed paws and shook my head. "No disrespect, Alejandro. I'm just used to, um.... When James and I, errr...." I trailed off and bit my lip while I followed him through the open door of his apartment.

He rolled his eyes with a growl. "Look, if I cared what you and your boyfriend did, I'd have asked him to come over for this little favor too." He shrugged and threw his shirt at a mostly full laundry basket sitting near the hall. "I said it before already, cabrón: I'm not making you do chit you don't want." My landlord's golden eyes had a frisky glitter to them, and I knew that it hadn't been an accident that he was working out in the yard all day. "You can leave now if you want, but don't expect any favors from me, man." He padded over to the door which was still open a crack and held it open. "You do something for me and I do something for you—that's how this works." A smile started to cross his muzzle and the tip of his tail started to wag back and forth while he reached down and undid the button on his jeans.

I looked from his eyes to the thick tented bulge in his pants. His scent was a lot stronger now that he'd taken off his shirt, but for some reason it was getting easier to handle; some of the musky notes even got my sheath going. Well, fuck it. I needed the time to get more money together, and he needed to get off.

At least Alejandro was pretty good looking.

I tucked my right arm through my shirt and slipped it off. "Fine, a deal's a deal. Let's do this."

A smirk crossed Alejandro's pointy muzzle while he kicked the door closed and flicked the lock shut. "Good choice, Remmy. Now let's have some fun." Immediately he turned and lunged, backing me into the couch and pinning me down there. "Remember the deal though: yu get one chance to say stop if I get too rough, but I get tah do whatever da fuck I want."

I gulped when I looked up at him and nodded softly. "Yeah, I won't waste it."

Alejandro showed a bit of tooth from the left corner of his muzzle and rolled his eyes. "Don' be a nerd, Remmy. Jus' tell me yes or no."

Some of his drool leaked onto the fur around my collar and I didn't dare say anything about it. The intensity in his eyes made me want to back away, but something deep inside me started to catch fire. "Yes... yes, sir." I folded my ears back and felt my cheeks burn with heat.

A grin wide enough for a crocodile stretched over my landlord's muzzle, and he eyed me up and down before lunging at me in a way I didn't expect. "That's what I like to hear—now sniff this." A hot, musky crease of fur enveloped my muzzle, and I screwed my eyes shut, letting out a surprised squeak. The athletic coyote above me let out a snarl. "C'mon, nutrito, sniff it.... What's it like smelling a real man, hmmm?"

Most of me cried out in protest; this was so rank, and he was being way rougher than anyone had ever been with me. I tried to push away from his armpit, but he was holding me there so tightly and eventually I would have to breathe. I struggled, just breathing through my mouth for a few seconds, but then I felt a row of claws rake through the fur along my back threateningly, and I took in a deep whiff through my nose, and to my surprise, a loud moan came out of my mouth.

Everything came together in that moment: that raw, rugged scent, those athletic arms holding me there and making me do things I didn't know I wanted. I lunged deeper into the thick tuft of fur in Alejandro's underarm and took in another deep breath. I felt a shiver go down my spine and the whole length of my thick tail. All of a sudden, he pulled me out from under his arm and sat up with his right paw planted gently on my collarbone. "So watchu think... bitch?" The corner of his muzzle curled up in a cheeky grin, and there was a mean glitter in his eyes.

I whimpered and pinned my ears back further, bringing my tail in to protect myself a bit, but for some reason I missed being pinned down. I wanted it again, I wanted to get used, but I could never admit that to him. I felt my eyes get watery for some reason which was weird with how turned on I was getting. "That was kinda rough...."

He rolled his eyes again and did a *tsk-tsk* motion with his left paw. "I told yu, you know I don't bullchit." He leaned in and brought his slender muzzle up to my ear, panting heavily while he slid his left arm down to free his stiff red cock from his faded blue briefs. His hot breath across my neck sent a shiver all the way to the tip of my tail, and the heat from his intense yellow gaze was just as potent as the pent up heat I felt dripping from the tip of his cock onto my navel. "Now tell me how yu really felt, Remmy. If you don't lie, yu might even have a little more fun doing this."

I looked away from Alejandro and whimpered again. He could smell how turned on I was, feel it as clear as day through the tent in my boxers where it pressed into his thigh. I thought about what I could say to get it over quickly, figure out the quickest path to the shower and a way of getting back to things like normal with James, but the words left my muzzle totally out of my control. "I want more...."

In another shocking instant, I felt the slender coyote's weight leave my body, and I thought for a bit that he'd show me a hidden video camera. He'd pull up a recording of what I'd just said on his phone and hit the send button. What actually happened was even more shocking though. A muscular, calloused footpaw landed square over my muzzle, and I screwed my eyes shut. When nothing hit me very hard, I slowly opened my eyes and realized that I'd been holding my breath. When I breathed in, a strong, heady smell like cheese and dirt and leather shot into my nose like a spear. My filthy coyote landlord was standing over me with a shark-toothed grin, and he only had three words.

"Lick it, slut."

I squeezed out a healthy gob of dish soap into the dirty wok and started scrubbing away all of the stuck pieces of chicken and mushrooms. I didn't tell James anything about what happened in Alejandro's apartment. Sure, I was a bit ashamed of it, but not enough to deny how much I liked it....

We talked, cooked some stir fry for dinner, and put on a couple episodes of something before he dug himself into his laptop and did some gaming while I did the dishes.

I felt an arm around my waist while I finished rinsing the wok and was about to move it to the drying rack. I yelped almost dropped it onto my feet. "J... James. Didn't I tell you I hate it when you sneak up on me?"

The cute, naïve face of a familiar red fox looked back at me with his paws raised apologetically. "Sorry, boo, I got done with my raids early, and I saw you were done with dishes." He kissed my right ear and brought his long black gloved arm tighter around me, letting his pads tease a little lower by my inner thigh. "I know shit's been stressful, so I was thinking we could have a little fun before you need to get to bed."

I had to hold back a bit of a groan. "I don't know about tonight, hon." I let out a sigh instead. "I was making calls for Tracy all day, we just got done with dinner and everything, and I've gotta get to class at seven. I'm tired, foxy." Sex was always such an amazing idea if James came up with it, but he was always too tired from the coffee shop or already planned a raid in his dumb online game or needed dinner and a shower when I asked for it.

James' chocolate-brown ears folded down sadly. "I guess things did get pushed kinda late." He leaned in and nuzzled up against my cheek. "If you're gonna be in bed soon, I could come in for a bit, maybe just put my muzzle to work and make it worth your while."

I shrugged and forced a smile, turning towards the hall and brushing my tail over his leg. "Not sure how I could say no to that. Thanks, dear, I'll make it up to you soon."

James licked his lips with a wicked grin while he led the way to bed. "Don't worry about it—it's just what I've gotta do for my significant otter."

Even though his bad pun half killed the mood for me, I still went along with him. This was still my apartment after all. James was still my boyfriend, and nothing needed to change or get screwed up if I didn't want it to. At least that was what I tried telling myself over and over while I kicked off my pants and flicked on the bedside lamp.

I lay on my back with my legs spread out wide, and James made his way over and started to run his pads over my thighs and to my navel, sometimes reaching over to stroke my half-hardness. "Yeah... there's my frisky otter. How's that feel, boo?"

"Mmmm." I shifted underneath his paws, not because I felt anything particularly amazing, but because I could barely feel anything that James was doing. It was frustrating, I wanted him to grip me with those sleek toned arms, dig his claws into me, and ask me to beg. I wanted him to hold me down, hold a vibrator to my sheath through my boxers, and then make me wear them over my face for cumming in my underwear like a little slut.

Thinking through these things was getting me really worked up. I felt my heart racing, and the tent in my boxers was almost painful. I shivered when I felt cool air hit the tip of my cock, and the anticipation built, even though James was slipping my boxers down so carefully it was like he was unpacking a nuclear fuel rod.

I heard the sound of a thin vulpine tongue dragging across a set of pawpads and felt them closing around my cock a few seconds later. James started to stroke around my tip in circles, and he grinned as he looked from my cock back up to my face. "Yrrf, you're really eager tonight." He gave my cock a few tugs and leaned in, letting his tongue flick over my tip while he fumbled with his own stiffness through his briefs.

I shifted and tried pumping my hips to get a little more stimulation, but James bobbed his head to cancel out the motion. I started to breathe heavier, not because I was really feeling anything but because I was starting to get frustrated. "Bring your h...hips up here.... I wanna taste."

He looked a bit surprised but brought his hips over anyways. "Guess you were in the mood for a bit more than me just taking care of you, hmm?" James stroked my ear gently between his warm pads and gave the base of my hardness a bit of a squeeze. Why the hell couldn't he grab me by the ears and force me down onto his cock and tell me to suck it?

The more we went along, the more playing rough just came to me as the natural thing. His russet and white thighs came into view, divided up nicely by his pointy red tip poking out of his sheath.

I sucked in a deep breath and let my eyes close when I leaned in closer. I tried to tease out the things I'd liked in James' scent before... what I always said I loved about him when we started dating. I felt a weight growing in my chest, the only thing that went through my mind was how annoyingly clean he was. I froze when I took in another whiff, and then I felt my eyes getting wet and a weight fill my chest. Without anything else I could do, I just sat up, looked him right in the eye and blurted it out: "I fucked the landlord."

James froze and a choked gasp that sounded like a slow motion cough came from his muzzle. His ears pressed flat, and I could already see tears starting to run down his cheeks. "So that's where you had to be when I was getting in from work." He whipped his head around and grabbed for some tissues from the nightstand. "Why would you lie to me about getting more gigs? I was putting so much extra time in at the coffee shop for us."

I felt my lip curl up in a snarl, and I whirled around, the last of my politeness was broken. "Don't be stupid, James. Even if you were actually working for as long as you claim to be, a couple extra hours at minimum wage don't do shit." He flinched and gave me a look like a hurt puppy, but I'd had it. "We had all the chances in the world to let Paul stay in the guest room, but you were so fucking confident that I'd be playing The Greek next weekend and that you'd get a gig at the Palladium after being showered in coffee tips for letting a bit of ankle show around pride." I noticed that I'd been getting louder and louder, and I reached for my undies with a groan. "I swear to god, James, you've got your head so far in the clouds. You want to be a perfect couple who stays exclusive, but you also want to show off, you whine about wanting more money, but you also can't think of doing anything but being a barista at Mount Rainier Coffee for the rest of your career."

James bit back with a bit of a snarl and smacked his paw down on the coffee table. "I like trying to meet new people—go ahead and throw me in jail for that." He sniffled and glared at me before ducking down to pull out something from under the bed. "Two customers told me they wanted to hear me sing. That's a lot better than my cheating boyfriend who wants me to just give up." He put the suitcase out on the bed and zipped it open.

I sighed and laid my head in my paws while the fox packed his suitcase. "Nothing actually works that way, James. I told you that when we moved here. Do you think you're the only barista who wants to sing on Broadway or act? It's not like there isn't a trope around here about the server with big dreams."

He raised his voice and almost screamed. "You're a dick." He zipped his bag shut and swiped one of his button downs from the closet. "You win. I admit that I fucked up. Do you think that gives you free rein to do whatever you want?"

I raised my voice. "What the fuck do you think I was doing, James? Do you think this was for fun?" I turned away from him and threw on a shirt and a pair of shorts. I felt tears threatening to come out. "I did what I did to keep a roof over our head. It didn't mean anything but...."

James shut his suitcase with a snap and glared at me with a snarl. "What, Remmy? What the hell could you possibly say to make me forgive you for doing that?"

That was it. "But I don't even want your shitty forgiveness

anymore." I had my eyes on the floor, but I whirled around to face the fox. "I have been doing nothing but work my ass off for us... for you. You begged me to help get you out here to stop being long distance, and I did that. You said that you would take your job seriously after I helped you land the interview, but I still get calls from my uncle Thomas about you talking with customers so long that their coffee goes cold. I ask you to cut back on water use, maybe consider getting a roommate to help pay rent. Then you take showers that are twice as long and break the deal with the roommate behind my back." He opened his mouth to protest, but I put up my paw and kept going. "And you broke the deal why? Did I cheat on you with him? Did he do something to hurt or take advantage of either of us? No, you kicked Paul out because we fell asleep on the couch together in a way that you thought was too cuddly."

James' ears were pressed flat, his suitcase had fallen on the floor, and he was biting his lower lip to hold back the anger I saw in his eyes. "This is just like you. Fuck you, Remmy. You're so holier than thou that you can't even see that you're just a fucking asshole."

I scoffed and leaned towards him, raising my voice again. "Yeah, I'm an asshole alright. You know what else James? I'm an enabler too. I enable this kind of shit for so long that I need to turn into an asshole to finally get anyone to listen." I backed off and put a paw over my chest while James stood and left the bedroom without any words, carrying his suitcase with him.

I followed James to the front door. He unlocked it and pulled it open, tail drooping but his hackles bristled all the way up. He turned to me with a look in his eyes like I had just gotten done beating him. "I'm going to LAX now and flying home. I hope you're happy, prick—you fucking ruined the life that I wanted."

A stab of guilt ran through me, but I was too pissed off to care. I looked him in the eyes without flinching, and I had a bit too much of a grin on my muzzle. "I fucked the landlord, and I'm gonna fuck him again because it was the best fucking sex I've had in three years."

I made a batch of pad thai with a few leftover veggies and not enough peanuts. When I was finally able to sit down and eat, someone knocked on the door. I rolled my eyes when I stood up to answer it. "I swear to god, James, it's been two days. If you're already trying to crawl back in like nothing happened...." I pulled open the door and paused. "Oh, hey, Alejandro."

My scruffy coyote landlord was dressed in his polo shirt and jeans, again with a bottle of something under his arm and a bit of a smirk on his muzzle. "I guess that wasn't for me."

I sighed and leaned up against the open door. "Yeah, that wasn't for you. You probably heard what happened."

Alejandro's smirk faded and his ears rolled back. "I heard enough." A bit of a smile came back to his muzzle, and he gave a bit of a chuckle. "Dios mío, I got four different noise complaints on Friday."

I should've been annoyed with that, but I started chuckling too. "Yeah, it was a shitshow." I laughed along with him for a bit and then reached back to scratch the back of my neck. "Um... really? Four? Sorry about that."

Alejandro shrugged. "Eh, chit happens man. Not like the landlord's gettin mad wit'chu. I hear he's a pretty cool guy."

I rolled my eyes and gave him a bit of a smack on the shoulder. "Yeah, I hear he's a pretty cool guy too. Not that I'd know though, I just get a dirty coyote who always walks around pretending to be landlord."

That made Alejandro's tail wag and he gave a throaty laugh. He pointed a claw at me. "'Chit man, you too? We gotta look out for this coyote sucio, I wonder what other travesuras he's gettin' into." He kept on laughing way longer than I did, but I was just enjoying watching this totally new side of him.

I shrugged and smiled. "I'll keep my eyes on him for sure. Want to come in? I can start looking out for that coyote right away."

"Yeah, sure, man." Alejandro paused and curled his ears back, taking a look back over his shoulder before following me in. He was totally silent until the front door closed, and he had a bit more heaviness in his voice when he saw my single plate of half-finished food and an empty spot on the table where the picture of me and James used to be. He settled into a chair next to the one where I'd been eating dinner solo. "So I take it things are over with the fox."

I made my way over to the kitchen with my bowl. "Yeah, we aren't much of anything anymore, but honestly we probably should've broken up a while ago." I topped off my bowl with some noodles from the wok on the stove. "I needed him when I was getting through college, and he wanted to come to LA and try to make it." I grabbed another bowl from the kitchen cabinet and filled it with the rest of the pad thai. "I just saw that we had some pretty different ideas of what we wanted after we got together." I brought both bowls back to the kitchen table and set one of them in front of Alejandro with a spoon and fork. "Ironically enough, him getting jealous for me passing out on top of our roommate Paul was what made me call in our little favor to pay for rent."

"*Chingada...* sounds like he had a lotta nerve. At least we were able to have a little fun." Alejandro looked down at the pad thai and then back up at me. "Oh thanks, Remmy, I haven' had Thai food in years." He took a couple bites of the noodles and scratched his chin for a moment. "Paul... I think I remember him. Was he tha cute torro um... buul that used to come over on weekends?"

I sat down and started eating again. "Yeah, that's him. I was starting to resent James around the time that Paul came by." I flashed Alejandro a grin and felt some heat fill my cheeks. "I can finally say how much I wanted to get into bed with that literal beefcake."

I saw the coyote's predatory grin for the first time since Friday, and his tail wagged with some excitement. "Boy, you sure missed a good time." He licked his lips and growled hotly. "Fuck, he was good in bed. I was so pissed when he stopped coming by to fuck around on Sundays."

A bunch of pieces started to fit together in my head. "Oh, so that was why he had to always leave so early and why you were...."

Alejandro nodded. "Why I was so hard-up when we were doing things." He chuckled and adjusted the tent in his pants while he stood up to take his bowl to the sink. "Like I said—when I knew I wouldn't get that sweet piece of ass this weekend, I was a little pissed off." He put out his paw to take my bowl. "That was a good time to do me a little favorito. Now can I take your trastes to the sink?"

I had to adjust my sheath a bit, and I gulped while I let him take my bowl, suddenly very conscious that I was cooking and eating without any pants. "Yeah, sure, thanks for taking the dishes up." My nostrils flared, and I caught a whiff of that same earthy musk that I'd gotten to know so well just a few days ago.

Alejandro took a few seconds too long to reach over me and grab my bowl, and I could see the subtle way he was rolling his hips, daring me to get a bit closer to the throbbing tent in his tight jeans.

I wrapped an arm around his waist and plunged my nose into the musky fabric with a moan, panting and taking in his raunchy canine funk just fine through two layers of fabric. "Oh fuck, I missed this." A firm, brown furred paw gripped the back of my head and pushed me in deeper, and I moaned again, reaching down to start stroking myself through my boxerbriefs. I was just getting drawn in deeper, wanting more, wanting to put my muzzle at the root of where his masculine musk was coming from. I could feel the outline of his knot starting to slide out, smell the precum that was starting to leak from his tip. I felt my thick tail swishing, and I started to pant with lust when I felt Alejandro's paw let up on my head. He was probably going to undo his jeans.

Instead of letting his pants drop, Alejandro reached a paw under my chin and tilted my head up so I could look him in the eye. "Cochino, at least let me do the dishes first." He had the biggest grin on his muzzle that I'd seen all night.

I whimpered and nodded, backing off while he took the dishes to the kitchen. He turned on the tap and started scrubbing. "So I got another deal for you, nutrito. You wanna hear it?"

I shook my head to clear it and sat up in my chair to try and push back the needy throbbing between my legs. "Yeah, sure, let's hear it."

I heard a clink from the dish rack while he finished up. "I know rent for a few months is gonna be rough for yu, plus things are a little lonesome in my apartamento." He dried his paws on the dish towel and made his way back to the table. "I move in here and you get your bull friend to join." He paused gave me a wink. "And the only rent you need to pay is groceries and utility."

I brought a paw to my chest and looked Alejandro right in the eye. "You'd do that for me? Hang on, you're not wanting to get together with me or anything, are you?"

He let out a hearty laugh and reached down next to his chair to bring out that bottle he'd brought with him and a couple of greenish shot glasses. "Naw, man, I've been off the boyfriend market for years now. Even if the familia would accept that, you're my friend and you don't go all romántico with your friends where I come from." He uncorked the bottle with the black tophat on it and filled both glasses, gesturing for me to take one of them. "So whachu say, chulo? Do we got a deal?"

I stood from my chair and took the glass, raising it up to Alejandro before bringing it to my lips and tipping it back. "Tenemos un trato."

He almost spat out his tequila but managed to get it all down. "La chinga? You didn't tell me you spoke Spanish."

I grinned and walked up to him, curling my thick tail around his waist. "I grew up in Van Nuys—of course I speak Spanish." With the best growl I could come up with, I brought my muzzle down to the warm crease of the coyote's chest and took in a bit of his scent. "Now that we've got a deal, why don't we get back to what we were doing?"

Alejandro brought one arm through his shirt and tossed it off without even needing to move me back. "Tenemos un trato." He growled and brought me in close, my nose met the scruffy brown fur between his lean pecs and I breathed in deep. I felt a firm, playful paw slide down my side and start to grope at my sheath. I tensed and let out a loud squeak when the coyote's teeth closed playfully around my ear, and I was already bucking my hips into his rough, calloused pads.

He let out a short playful snarl when I reached down to undo the button of his jeans. I popped them open and slid them down by the zipper in one quick motion. Alejandro's arms loosened up around me, and he sighed happily at having his cock finally able to breathe a bit.

That scent hit my nose like a tidal wave, and I licked my lips while I led Alejandro to the couch and pushed him back so I could bury my muzzle into the hot crease between his sheath and his sack.

I stopped when I was just a couple inches away from getting what I wanted. "Really? Fucking really, Alejandro?"

He sneered and started giggling. "Something wrong, Remmy?"

I rolled my eyes and put a paw on either side of his hips and yanked off the turquoise pair of boxerbriefs he had on. "Don't play dumb with me, mentiroso. I knew my undies weren't that easy to lose."

He struggled a bit, but not enough to tear them or cause any damage. "Aww, c'mon, Remmy, I was gonna give 'em back when we got done here."

I gave them a bit of a sniff and grinned. "Well... they do smell like you now. Alright, I forgive you." I tossed them aside and lunged back in with a growl, pressing my nose up against the base of his sheath and letting my tongue brush over whatever it touched. Alejandro started to sit up to say something, but I reached up his chest and pinched his right nipple, and he fell flat on his back with a yip and a groan.

I was using my other paw to stroke myself through the tent in my boxerbriefs and though the coyote was wagging his tail and bucking his hips, he didn't seem as into it as when he made me "worship" him last time. I reluctantly pulled back from that musky sheath and gave the leaky pointed tip of his cock a lick. "Something wrong?"

Alejandro was panting and looking down at me with a hunger in his eyes that was... needy? "I was usin' your chonies to put over my nose when I was pawin' off all weekend after we had our fun." He growled and wimpered again and stared between my legs. "I think I need somewhere to put my muzzle."

It was my turn to grin then, and I lifted my leg to straddle my filthy coyote landlord. I used my tail to slide off the boxers I was wearing and lowered my hips so whatever he wanted was right in reach of his muzzle. "I like the way you think, coyote sucio. Let's make a mess." I licked my paw and started to stroke along the entire length of his throbbing crimson shaft, rubbing the pad of my thumb over his pointy tip and using the webbing between my fingers to squeeze and tug on his thick juicy knot.

I felt Alejandro's pointy muzzle pressed into my taint, his nose angled upwards to catch a good whiff from my balls. Then I felt his thin, warm tongue gently probing its way further back, sliding into the tight ring under my tail.

I gasped and let out a frantic squeak, pressing my hips back and thrusting into the leathery pawpads that had just closed around my cock. Everything was breathless and frantic, a frenzy of thrusting, licking, sniffing, and stroking. I'd practically licked away everything the coyote had to offer under his sack, but I still had his sheath. I craned my neck and pressed forward, still pumping his throbbing cock hard while my muzzle met the thick mound of fur around his maleness.

I could feel myself getting close—movements were fluid and sensations came in waves. The only solid things were that tenacious, masculine musk that overpowered everything and the rapidly building pressure at the base of my cock. "F... fuck, I never want to get this smell off of me." I arched my back and panted while white stars exploded behind my eyes and thick strands of warm, silky cum pumped from the tip of my cock.

Alejandro let out a loud yipping howl and shivered below me. I could feel a few splashes from him matting down the fur around my navel and I tilted my head up, closing my eyes and moaning while I let him paint my face with his thick spunk.

We lay there breathlessly for a bit, just panting and enjoying the warm high after another intense round. When I finally opened my eyes, I saw the turquoise pair of boxerbriefs that he'd stolen last time really close by on the floor, and I snatched before he could and used it to wipe some of the cum off of my face.

Alejandro grinned and chuckled. "See? Told you I was giving 'em back."

I threw them at him with a smirk when I was done wiping my face clean. "It's not about the undies, smartass. It's about you stealing shit from me. Am I gonna regret letting you move in?"

Alejandro took a big sniff of them and put them back on the bed. "Ehh, they smell too much like me for me to get off with 'em anymore. Besides, I've got you around now, chulo."

I rolled my eyes and smirked. "Yeah, true, I am kinda stuck here now." I wrapped my tail around Alejandro's waist playfully, and I was about to go in for another whiff from his chest when I heard my phone ringing.

I picked up without even thinking. "Yeah, it's Remmy."

A deep, familiar voice that suddenly put me in the mood for a round two came over the line. "Hey, dude, it's Paul. Look, I know that there was a lot of drama with James." There was a long pause, and I glanced over to Alejandro. He gestured in the shape of a pair of bull horns, and I nodded and gave him a thumbs up. Paul kept going. "Listen man... I get if this is awkward I just wanted to call and let you know I still wanna be friends. I just—I'm calling 'cause I had a really shit weekend and I, um... you got time to hang out soon?"

Alejandro couldn't hear anything, so he was squirming next to me like a kid at the county fair who really needs to go pee. "What's he saying? Chit, man, does he wanna hook up wit'chu?"

I was holding back a giggle while I pushed Alejandro back from trying to take the phone from me. "Dude, shut up, shut the hell up, man." I tried to whisper away from the phone.

Paul cleared his throat a bit nervously. "Uh... is it a bad time Remmy? I could text you or call back later."

I gave Alejandro a playful shove and he fell off the end of the couch with a yip. I had to cough a couple times so I wasn't giggling while I talked to Paul. "Naw, man, tonight's great actually. Long story but we won't need to worry much about James. I've already got a friend over so having you by is no biggie."

I could almost hear Paul perk up on the other end of the line. "Awesome, can't wait to see you. But uh... with James, I...."

"Ehh, don't worry about it, Paul. I'll tell you when you get here. Long story short: things can work like we planned them again. We've just got a different other roommate."

"Who's he?"

I grinned and swatted at Alejandro with my tail when he tried to grab my phone again. "Oh, just some mangy coyote who lives in the complex. He's a pretty cool guy, and he was getting a little bored and lonely in an apartment by himself."

"Sounds like pretty convenient timing. It'll be nice to meet him."

Alejandro sat up on his knees and wrapped his paw around his half hard cock, bucking his hips and thrusting into it while his tongue lolled out of his muzzle. I grinned while I responded to Paul. "Oh, trust me, he's excited to meet you too."

I must've come off a little bit horny with that comment because there was a bit of a longer pause than normal and I could swear that Paul was adjusting his pants or something. "Yeah, uhh, so I need to shower off and get a bite to eat, but then I should be by in about an hour."

I started to stroke my stiffening cock, and I dropped my voice to be as sultry and teasing as I could manage. "Don't worry, just come over. We've got some pad thai on the stove, and you'll probably want to wait until later to shower."

TOUCH

The Things We Do

Tarl "Voice" Hoch

(*CW: dubious consent*)

The night air tasted like fried circuits each time Xe took a breath, and for the hundredth time that night, they questioned what they were doing in this part of town so late at night. Foot nervously tapping on the ground, they glanced at the hyena across from them as he motioned towards the alleyway they both stood in front of.

"And that's it. Once you come back out and I report to the Trinity of One, you're in."

Xe shook their head, raising a delicate paw to push one of their ears away from their face. "Really Zain, that's it?" They motioned to the alley. "All I have to do is go into an alley in the middle of the night in one of the worst sectors of New Seattle. Machines above, anyone or anything could be down there. Don't you read the feeds? Weird shit is happening all over town. Weird cults, eldritch rites, it's like something from a horror vid."

Something let out a cry in the distance followed by the eerie wail of corporation security sirens rising and falling like a wounded machine. Zain gave the distinct laugh of his species and turned his head so his augment eye gazed at Xe. The lapin could hear the whir of the outdated cybernetics as it processed the data it took from scanning them. "Look, you wanted into the gang. We all took some kind of test, one way or another. It's based off a number of factors that the Trinity of One comes up with through data they glean from whoever is trying to join the gang." The hyena took a drag off his stim-stick, the leather of his jacket creaking with the movement. With his free paw, he motioned to Xe's body with a meaty finger, stopping when it came to the lapin's crotch.

"And let's be real for a moment, *Chad*—"

Xe hissed: four sets of sharp chrome canines sliding down beside his buck teeth with an audible click. "I told you *never* to use my old name!"

"Yeah, yeah, sure thing, Xe." Zain took another drag from his stim-stick before motioning again to the rabbit's body. "Not many gangs want to take on a Null as a member. At best, all your kind can expect is to be the group's fuck toy and then tossed to the curb, maybe even with a few credits *if* you're lucky."

Xe snarled at the hyena, fangs bared, unshed tears welling in their eyes. "You know I don't like that term!" They took a step forward, fingers curling into fists. The hyena raised a paw and shook hi

Zain shook his head. "Come on Xe, how long have we known each other. You know I don't mean it like that."

The rabbit's artificial fangs clicked back into their sheaths as Xe ran his paws over their body. The bodysuit they wore resembled something that was a cross between a feminine white one-piece swimsuit and a pair of black booty shorts that hugged close enough to the lapin's tight body that one could see the distinct smoothness there. Black arm sleeves and a pair of black thigh-high boots with white highlights completed the outfit. The cream colour of the lapin's fur gave the outfit an almost fetish nun appearance, broken only by how the rabbit's ears fell on either side of their head. They almost resembled an archaic women's hairstyle, even though the lapin kept their hair as androgynous as possible.

Zain grunted, and Xe could smell the heavy scent of arousal coming from him, despite the stim-smoke that coated the hyena. Xe had given themselves up to Zain a couple times, mostly because they liked how the hyena's paws felt when they caressed their fur, and how he never held back, despite knowing Xe's past.

But what topped it for Xe was that the hyena didn't care about the rabbit's lack of breasts or hips, and could still enjoy taking his release in the limited ways the rabbit could provide. The lapin shivered and made a soft noise in the back of their throat. Zain let out another barking laugh.

"See what I mean? I mean, be proud of your body, sure, you spent enough on it going through the change. I personally wouldn't; could never get rid of Zain Jr, but that's me. I would have rather spent those creds on new wet-ware and maybe some new chrome. You've always been a bit... odd, even when we were kids. But now here we are. The Trinity of One said you needed to go down this alley: To the end mind you. There's no negotiating, no lying your way out of it, no nothing. You come back out, and I tell the Trinity of One you passed. *If* you come out." He grinned, flashing a mix of gold and silver teeth.

"So you keep saying." Xe's foot tapping increase in tempo. "One test?"

"One test."

"And I am in."

"You're in."

"And not as a fuck toy." Xe met Zain's gaze.

"Right. An actual member."

The rabbit's foot stopped its beat, and they took a deep breath. Stealing a glance at the gaping maw of the alleyway, they traced the old brickwork and faded graffiti that marked it. No one built with brick anymore, and how this section of town remained unmodeled was nothing short of a miracle. Probably a good thing since any metal would have probably succumbed to the cancer of rust by now. Still, there was something that just felt... old about the place, and made Xe's foot want to start tapping again.

Taking a deep breath, the rabbit turned to face the alley. "Really wish I had your eye right now, Zain."

The hyena laughed. "It wouldn't do you any good. I can see only a few feet in. It's almost like the shadows are fighting my augment." He laughs. "Silly, right?"

Xe let out a half-hearted chuckle before taking a deep breath and letting it out slowly, bringing their paws to their chest in a half-prayer. Zain rolled his eyes but held his tongue. He'd seen weirder things than someone reaching out to the divine. When Xe finally lowered their paws, Zain reached out to his friend.

"Here, take this."

The rabbit opened their delicately fingered paw under Zain's, and something slight dropped into it. "Wh… why?" Xe finally asked when their gaze fell on the small pen knife in their paw.

"Just take it. I know you aren't a fan of arming yourself, but…" Zain shrugged, averting his eyes for a moment. "and I know this isn't the *Partition…*" Xe winced, and Zain raised his paws, palms outwards. "Not that I would ever put you in that situation again, but… damn it, just take it."

Xe bit their bottom lip with their buck teeth before bowing. "Thank you, Zain. Really." Turning back to the alley, the rabbit pocketed the knife. There came a distinct crack of a glowstick being activated, and a soft neon pink glow softly illuminated Xe as they started walking into the shadows, a paw raising to brush something aside that Zain couldn't see. The hyena watched as their friend slowly was swallowed up by the darkness, patting themselves down before finding another stim-stick and placing it between his lips. Using electrical current from the pinkie finger on his right paw, he activated it and took a deep breath until the stims coated his lungs. Holding it, he let out a long blast of pollutant.

"Good luck, Xe. You're going to need it…"

The vibration was subtle. It caressed me like the faintest breeze, not that I had felt such a thing hidden away as I have been all these years. Yet there it was, teasing along the hairs of my limbs, the light dance of fairy feet half-imagined. I shifted, only slightly. The movement felt glorious after so long spent immobile, waiting. I could not see anything in my home, but I could feel it now.

There.

In the distance, a faint delicate tread. A light vibration that lifted off the ground and hummed around me. I shifted again for the sheer pleasure of movement, the barest movement of a leg, just to remember what it felt like.

Soon.

I couldn't remember what day it was, what month, what year even. Once upon a time there had been things such as snow, rain, to help tell the passage of time. But no longer. The world had changed so much since I had come here to this city. Others like me were here, I could feel them every so often, a vibration in the metropolis. A bright line of touch against an ever present hum of artificial noise. A hint of the divine in a world of the mundane.

Soon the others would feel me move and would rejoice to know I was alive.

But not yet.

I had to wait.

Thankfully I've had years of practice.

I settled in to wait.

Xe paused, their eyes straining against the edge of the glowstick's light, trying to see beyond. They had been walking for what seemed like half an hour or so, but knew it was probably significantly less. "Sure Xe, if you had caved and bought some chrome, you wouldn't be in this mess. A simple chromometer would have helped a lot right now." They chuckled. "Except you'd be staring at what time it was in the corner of your eye forever, unless you paid extra to shut the program off. Who seriously wants to know what time it was at every waking moment of their life anyway?"

Running their free paw against their neck they rotated it. There had been a time when it would have clicked or cracked, but after they had upgraded their wetware the joints moved like a well oiled machine. As close as Zain was to Xe, even he didn't know just how often the lagomorph had gone under the knife. Their transition to gender ambiguity had been one of the more visually drastic changes, sure, but there had been so much more. Ever since the night at *Partition*, Xe had made a promise to themselves. One was that they would be true to themselves. The other was that they wouldn't let their species be a hinderance to them anymore.

Shaking their head to clear the lingering chill those memories sent racing along their spine, Xe pushed their forward-facing ear away from their eyes so they could get a better look around them. The walls were still brick, and Xe reached out, brushing two fingertips along the coarse stone. It was a unique texture, one that seemed to stay with the rabbit even after they pulled their fingers away from the wall. Rubbing their fingertips together they felt slightly sticky, and Xe raised their fingers to their nose.

No scent.

That surprised the lapin as everything in the city had a scent. Usually of oil, metal or pollution; there was always a scent. Xe pressed the palm of their right paw against the brick, feeling the stone jab into the flesh with a hundred different pin pricks. They closed their eyes, and a grin dashed across their face. Pushing harder against the wall, the rabbit made a sound in their throat and grinned as the feeling intensified. Pain was one of the things Xe understood: it had been with them for so long. It was the brush of a lover, a gateway to their own transformation. It had seen them through so much.

Then with a sigh, Xe pulled back with a squelching noise. Strands of something seemed to cling to their palm and fingers, and Xe curled their fingers into a fist. The pinpricks of the wall were still sharp and lingering, but ultimately faded far too quickly. Opening their paw, Xe frowned as everything felt a bit tacky, though in the low light they couldn't quite make out why. Their nose wasn't helping either; whatever was causing the weird tactile sensation was far too subtle to be picked up.

"Weird," Xe whispered, brushing their paw off on their shorts, whatever was covering their paw finally coming off with a little vigorous rubbing. Turning to look back the way they had come, the rabbit was surprised to see that they couldn't see the light at the end of the alley. And gazing upwards didn't help either, as the buildings on either side of the alley seemed to stretch ever upwards. Not that that was such a weird thing in New Seattle, but the stark white, chrome and synthetics that coated buildings provided subtle light using various technologies. Here, everything was dark.

Xe shook their glowstick to try and mix the chemicals inside a bit more to give off more light. If it failed, they had a few more secreted in a pouch on their left hip, but after that they would be on their own. Given that the alley seemed to stretch on a lot further, Xe was pretty sure they didn't want to be in here longer than they thought they would have to be.

"At least it's a straight line…" they whispered to themselves. With a shake of their head, they continued on.

It was a constant hum now, the hairs on my body alight with each note. Whatever had entered my domain was slowly making its way closer to me, and I couldn't help but shift slightly at the thought. My senses were coming alive, speeding up after so long being near dormant. There was the urge to hunt, to take off down the alley, to stalk as my ancestors and distant relatives did.

But that wasn't my way.

So I let the humming come to me, the tremor against my hairs, the vibration echoing off the walls and ground. When the humming stopped, the urge to move screamed from my nerves, and I shifted my arms and legs. It wasn't much, maybe an inch or two, but I caught myself. Reining in my instincts I instead stretched my consciousness outwards.

Then came a crescendo of sensation as whatever was coming touched the wall of the alley. The feeling was like ecstasy as they pulled away, my body shivering ever so slightly at the wail of sensation. The movement felt delicate, which suggested a woman. But not.

I paused.

A woman would mean potential. The prospect brought parts of me awake, if only slightly. I hadn't felt the need to breed in a long time, so long in fact that the species on the receiving end didn't have to be one of my own. It would be less enjoyable, less thrilling, but it would scratch a very ancient need that burned in me now that I was thinking about it.

Yet the signals coming to me spoke of something else. Though the radius of heavy notes was smaller than I would take for a man, it was not small enough for a woman. And there was something in the way the touch had lingered that felt... off.

I stretched my mouth apart, hearing parts of it click as ligaments stretched and warmed up. It was getting nearer. Curiosity warred with hunger with each beat of its footsteps on the ground. With each vibration that rolled over my senses, things became sharper, clearer.

Whatever this creature approaching me was, I was ready.

Xe cracked another glowstick and shook it. In the birth of the new, stronger light, they looked around. The sky was no longer visible above them; instead it felt like there was something blocking out the night. The sounds were muffled, and the way that the sounds echoed off the walls seemed to become deadened as they raced skyward.

They pushed their ear from their face and moved closer to the wall of the alley. They weren't sure when it happened, but the walls were covered in a fine sheet of threads. It was as if someone had sprayed synthetic fibers across it in some kind of urban knitting or textile graffiti. Getting as close as they could, they sniffed it, surprised to find that it didn't have any sort of scent rather than a bit of dust. Reaching out, Xe pressed a blunt claw against the fabric. When he pulled back, it drew some of the strands with it. Cocking their head to the side, Xe started to place his paw on the fabric, but stopped short. Something didn't feel right about it. They remembered how tacky the wall had felt behind them, and this was clearly a thicker coating.

But of what?

Xe looked back the way they had come. "How bad do you want this, Xe? Is being a part of their gang really that important to you?"

They looked back towards the depths of the alley. Something was down there. They could feel it somewhere in their chest. A pressure that seemed to press against them, some sort of primal instinct. "All you have to do is touch the wall," Xe said to themselves. "That's it. Reach the end of the alley, that's it. Surely the Trinity of One wouldn't send me to my death."

Xe ran their free paw down their body, feeling the tightness of the muscles under their clothing, the smoothness of their pelt. Finally their paw came to rest on the cleft between their legs. "Even a Null like me.

"I am not afraid."

Xe started forward, paw clenched around the glowstick, their other in a fist. "I will prove to them I am not just some toy to be played with and discarded. I am not some weak prey animal who cowers in the bushes and lets the predators do what they will. I will do this. I will do this for me!"

They were so close.

So very close.

Another wash of sensation washed over my hairs, smaller than the first, but closer, heavier despite the lightness of touch. My instincts burned me, screaming at me to hunt, to leave my lair and find the interloper and feed; lust or hunger, it didn't matter.

But I fought it. I fought it and won. Curiosity pushed me to wait, to let the creature come to me. They could be armed; they could have weapons of light or fire. So I waited, surprise being the ultimate weapon of my kind. They would come to me, and I would have them.

There was light in the distance of the alley, coming ever closer. It was a soft glow, almost too bright after so long in the dark. But I welcomed the sensation of it entering my world, of what it meant to me for what it brought with it.

I felt their footsteps, each one falling upon me like a hammer blow of sensation. The feel of each step was as delicate as the touch on the wall, though with the same level of confusion to me as well. It read as feminine, but not. I could almost picture the movement of the creature's feet, legs, and hips in my mind, but the incoming information wasn't enough. I strained my eyes to see if I could see the being, but that had never been my kind's strong points.

Closer they came.

I shifted ever so slowly, rising myself up so I no longer rest on my nest. Only my legs and arms touched it now. The movement felt almost too good. Even better as I slowly made my way up the wall, easily finding places for my limbs as I rose upwards. The canopy I created over the alley was the perfect cover for me to move, to spring my trap.

The creature passed under me as I moved along the canopy. It was a rabbit from what I could see, and its form was pleasing to my senses and my decision was made. Shifting my position, I affixed a line to the canopy and slowly lowered myself behind the rabbit.

This was going to be fun.

Xe stared at the back of the alley, foot tapping a steady beat on the soft floor. Unlike the walls, the covering to the floor wasn't sticky, despite being a heavy version of the fabric that had covered the walls earlier. The walls were thick with it now as well, though Xe suspected it wouldn't be as lush as the threads under their feet. But what stood before them confused them.

It was clearly the end of the alley, though how they were to touch the wall felt impossible. Something had strung the synthetic fibers all over the place, building a sort of nexus point at the end of the ally. There were little bits and pieces of things strewn in the threads that made up the nest. A cred card, an old watch, a synthleather jacket, and even a few stim-sticks. They looked old by the amount of discolouration on them, and Xe only paid them a moment's notice.

Their eyes searched the nest, and finally they smiled, taking a step forward. Weaving between the low hanging threads of fabric, Xe arched their body and planted a paw against the only bare spot among the threads draping the wall. A smile broke across their face a moment before they pulled away from the wall. One of the low hanging threads brushed their shoulder, and Xe felt it tug on their fur. With a frown they tugged against the thread which pulled taut until finally letting go, taking some of Xe's fur with it. Taking a step back, Xe froze, their ear rising slightly.

Something had touched the soft fabric-coated ground

behind them.

Something big.

The rabbit didn't notice me while I slowly dropped down from the canopy, limbs stretched out to stabilize myself as I watched the rabbit reach out and touch the bare spot on the wall by my nest. The tug against the threads when it almost got itself tangled sent a heavy shiver along my body, the sensation having raced down the anchor thread I was lowered myself with.

As I touched the floor of the alley and raised myself up, the rabbit paused, ears moving slightly, before it turned to face me. I opened my mouth wide and spread my limbs.

Bask in my glory, little one!

"By the Corporations!" Xe took a step back, paws flying to their open mouth.

It was huge.

Spreading the entire span of the alley, the lapin's eyes struggled to take it all in. It was dark as the shadows surrounding it, all fangs and limbs.

Xe's foot rapid fired and beat the ground as they hunched down, eyes darting to find a way out. If they could just make a break for it, their natural and modified legs would easily take them away from here. They had touched the wall at the end of the alley.

The creatures lowered its front limbs, and Xe saw their change. With a shove of their legs, they were off. Time seemed to slow down as implanted bioengineering took over. Xe watched as they moved closer to the creature, its reactions far too slow as the rabbit moved towards the space under the arch of its left legs.

Xe's left foot hit the pavement and pushed, shooting them forward. *So close,* Xe's mind whispered. They saw every detail in the legs as they shot under them. They were hard, shell-like. There was something alien about them, reminding the lapin of late night holo-vids their sister and they had watched when they had been young while their parents were doing whatever parents did in VR.

They turned their head slightly, the corner of their vision catching the face of the beast as it turned in slow motion.

It's a spider.

The notion threatened to throw Xe off course. *How can something like that exist? It's impossible.* Their right foot hit the pavement and drove them forward under the first limb even as it closed downwards. This close, the size of the spider pushed against the lapin's mind. They didn't suffer from arachnophobia, but this was something else. Some primal drive screamed through all of their biological modifications and pushed them with animal fear.

Past the third and fourth leg, Xe's left foot slammed down, and they found their stride. Implanted fangs or not, the rabbit's natural defence had always been speed, and Xe always kept that in mind when choosing their bio-mods. Pound for pound they would never take someone like Zain or almost any of the members of the Trinity of One.

The corner of Xe's muzzle pulled in into a smile. *And it's all paid off. I'm going to have a word with Zain wh—*

Xe's right leg came down, and the lapin was thrown to the ground, the pavement rushing up too fast for them to brace. Their head rebounded off the concrete with a crack, their reinforced skull the only thing saving them from death. The lapin's right leg was on fire, and without having to look Xe knew something had torn, or broken.

"Fuck fuck fuck!" they screamed out, hammering a fist on the concrete.

Fangs slid from their sheath and glistening chitin claws unsheathed from the long bones of the rabbit's arms, the blades extending from their elbow as well as from synth skin ports in their palm. "Come on! You want me, come and get me!"

My suspicion of laying down fresh webbing when I had set down on the ground had been correct. The creature hadn't even noticed, too wrapped up in the glory that is my form. The strikes of its footfalls hitting the pavement had caught me by surprise, the feeling of each beat hitting me like a strike of a massive drum.

What was this thing? It looked to be a hare or rabbit of some sort, yet even now it changed shape, growing fangs of its own even as it lay crippled on the ground.

What have I missed in all these years?

I paused, watching it try to lift itself up, its right paw still held fast on the ground. I could feel its heartbeat even from here, a rapid-fire rhythm that was far too fast for anything living. If it kept up like this all I would have to do is wait and it would burn itself out.

Yet...

The feeling of lust rose again as I took a stride forwards. The creature bared its fangs at me, yelling out meaningless threats. I could see that its weapons are chitin, like my own, and I doubted they would be able to crack my body. Maybe a joint, but that was always the fear of my kind. To be hobbled until our next molt, and those came so rarely these days.

I decided this warranted a different approach for now.

"What.... Are.... You...?"

Xe fell silent mid-threat.

"What? What did you say?"

The massive spider shifted ever so slightly as fangs the length of Xe's arm moved. "What...are...you?"

Xe shifted their body, keeping their right arm slightly behind so they could throw a punch with their blades if need be. "My name is Xe. I am a rabbit."

"I find that hard to believe." The spider's words came smoother. One leg rose to point at the lapin's left arm, held at guard across their body.

Xe glared at the spider. "I find you hard to believe."

A grating sound filled the confines of the alley. "I am why you fear the darkness."

"I don't fear the darkness."

"Then what do you fear, little one?"

Xe laughed. "Dying in an alleyway to something that shouldn't exist takes the number one spot right about now."

Again the grating sound filled the alley, and Xe realized the creature was laughing. "You are an interesting one. Perhaps if you keep me entertained I will not eat you like I had planned."

"Excuse me if I don't believe you."

The spider's body lowered slightly, giving off an almost shrugging motion. "You can hardly barter in the position you are in."

Xe laughed. His uninjured foot starting to tap a rhythm on the ground. "May I ask you something, creature that shouldn't be?"

Lowering its head in a bow, the spider regarded Xe with its multitude of eyes. "You may."

Taking a deep breath and letting the pain suppressors fire within their body to try and cut the pain, Xe opened their eyes and regarded the monster before them. "How is it you can talk? Are you some kind of bio-engineering experiment gone wrong? Were you created in a Corporation lab? Or are you a radiation mutant that came in-city from the wastes?"

"I have always been, and always will be. My kind ruled this world when it was young. We are your gods and demons, the primordial spinners of fate, time and the circle of life."

Xe's foot stopped. "That sounds like a lot of shit if you ask me."

The spider took a step forward, lowering its face closer yet keeping out of reach of Xe's claws. "Why did you stop?"

"Stop what?" Xe asked while leaning back from the multitude of glassy black eyes.

"The rhythm. The vibrations. They have such an…" The spider's fangs stretched for a moment. "…excellent feel to them. Something I have never felt in this world."

Looking at their upraised foot, Xe cocked their head. "Pardon?"

"The rhythm, the beat, one of the countless vibrations of this world; yet so unique. You do not feel masculine or feminine, but you are a gender none-the-less. You create such an interesting pattern on this world, one I find more pleasing as it caresses my body."

Xe brought their foot down in a single blow on the

pavement, watching as the spider shifted ever so slightly. *Interesting.*

"Such sweet music to my senses. Tell me, what are you?"

The lapin shifted their body, managing to correct the angle of their leg so that the self-repairing cells could start to mend their flesh. Thankfully the pain suppressors were doing a fairly good job. It still hurt, but nowhere near what it had before. *It had lain webbing behind it when it snuck up on me.* Xe glanced at the thick thread glued to his entrapped foot. *I should have known. The signs were everywhere... I'm going to murder Zain if he knew about any of this.*

"You mean what gender am I?" Xe flicked their head to the side so their fallen ear moved out of their vision. "If you want to use the vulgar term, I am a Null."

"A *Null?*" The spider leaned back, and Xe felt it was looking elsewhere, though with so many eyes it was hard to tell where the thing was looking. After a moment it regarded them again. "Such an inadequate term for something that provides such a satisfying vibration to this world. What do you call yourself then?"

"I am genderless. Much like I assume you are."

The grating laughter echoed off the alley walls. "I am hardly genderless, little one. I am very much a man." It rose up, and Xe's muzzle fell open, for there where they would have expected hard carapace stood a very large penis. One that was very much erect like a telecom shaft aimed at the sky. *By the Corporations, even Zain isn't built like that. That thing is huge!* Xe swallowed, their foot starting to beat its rhythm again.

"You're a spider; how is that even possible? Spider's don't have...that!"

Laughing, the arachnid lowered itself back to all of its legs. "I told you, I am no ordinary spider. I am a god of the species, a supreme being that roams this world to watch the webs of fate."

"That makes no sense. You're supposed to have pedipalps. You're supposed to subdue your mates. You're... you're—"

"There are no females of my kind, little one. I breed with prey that I find... pleasing."

Xe's foot sped up, which caused the spider to take a step

closer. The rabbit shivered as visions of pregnant spiders with scores of squirming spiderlings in their swollen bellies threatened to overwhelm them. "That's... that's....—"

"Majestic. Yes."

"Horrific." *By the Corporations and the Great Code, thank you for not being able to bear children.*

The spider raised a leg and pointed it at Xe. "Birth is never horrific. It is beautiful, one of the most beautiful things from the beginning of time. I am surprised you are so ignorant, my genderless guest. You seemed far more sophisticated than that."

Xe took a couple deep breaths, trying to calm themselves down. Their heartrate had slowed slightly but was still going too fast. It was starting to make them sleepy and that was dangerous right now. Using various bio-feedback techniques the doctors and bio-shamans had taught them, the lapin tried to bring themselves back to equilibrium. "Well, for my species that sounds pretty horrific."

"You are a strange one indeed, little prey."

"What is your name?" Xe winced as the bones in his leg shifted to their proper alignment and started to knit. This wasn't their first broken bone, as some of the gangers liked their sex rough and tended to treat Nulls as Non-People. But they tended to leave clean breaks that mended fast. Their leg was anything but a clean break.

"I do not have a 'name'," the spider said, leaning closer. "What is yours?"

"Xe." Another wave of pain washed over the lapin, their foot rapid-fire on the concrete, each strike sounding like a muffled gunshot. Each echo vibrated up the wall, and the spider quaked with each blow.

"Such exquisite vibrations, Xe. I find them to be most agreeable."

Xe cocked their head to the side, a slow smile crossing their muzzle as the light from the fading glowstick twinkled in their eye. Carefully, they slowed their foot's beat on the ground to a steady rhythm, slow but also heavy. The spider's front legs waved in the air like a dog trying to learn how to swim. "You like that, don't you, Mr. Spider?"

The spider stopped its shiver and turned its gaze to Xe, fangs moving. "Why did you stop?"

"It just surprises me, that's all. I don't know why I didn't put it all together in the first place. But that might have been the pain suppressors… they tend to fuck with my judgement and cognitive skills."

"I repeat, why did you stop?"

"What does it feel like?"

Shifting, the spider rose its front two legs into the air, moving them about in such a way that it reminded Xe of a conductor they once saw on an old vid. "It feels like… Imagine a paw running along your fur, as I can only assume it feels. The strokes run from very light, a brushing of your guard hairs, to heavy, where they move the skin itself."

Zain's paw on my fur, running along it, exploring. The way he caresses the edge where I shaved it off to wear the skintight part of my outfits. The feel of him dancing a blunt claw along the naked skin, or the light growth. How he touches my whiskers, making my nose twitch more than normal… Xe's foot started up again, the beat completely different than before.

"You can imagine it, can't you?" The spider leaned forward, his massive fangs inches from Xe's face. The lapin's nose caught the scent of age and something dry. Their arm twitched but halted. The chitin blades retracted into their boney sheaths. Something told them even if they got a good strike in, they would be dead.

"I can." Xe nodded. "It sounds…pleasant. I take it you can't really hunt visually then?"

The spider moved side to side. "I can, though not well. Vibration is my world."

The lapin looked down at their leg, now fully healed. They felt sick and exhausted, their body having used up a lot of their inner resources to heal it. The spider seemed to notice, reaching out with a fore-claw to caress the rabbit's entrapped leg.

"Most interesting. My kind would do much to possess that ability."

"I know some doctors who could give it to you. I am sure they have seen weirder things than a giant arachnid."

The claw paused against Xe's leg. "No."

"Why not?"

"That would be sacrilegious."

Xe shook their head, brushing their ear away from their face. "Much of this world you would find sacrilegious then." The lapin averted their eyes for the briefest of seconds. "Do you find me so profane then? I did change my body after all."

"You have, and though the idea of changing my own body is repellent, your body is your own and thus your own to do whatever you desire to."

A gasp escaped Xe's muzzle in a flash, quickly covered up by a delicate paw. Shifting their head their ear fell back in front of their eyes, hiding them from the creature. "How noble of you," they whispered, a tear threatening to run down their cheek. *Remember where you are Xe… This thing could still eat you if it wanted. Does it want to?* Clenching and unclenching their fingers, Xe took a deep breath and raised their eyes back to the spider.

"You cry, little one," the spider said, the claw that had been caressing the rabbit's leg moving to brush aside the fallen ear. Large eyes sparkling with unshed tears greeted the multitude of onyx orbs. "Why?"

Xe brushed their eyes with the back of their arm and shook their head. "I will not tell you that story, Spider. My pain is not yours to share. But… thank you for your concern. It's more than others are willing to give my kind."

"Kneel and close your eyes."

The rabbit looked up for a moment, meeting the creature's many eyes. *This is it then, this is where I meet my end… Not in a fight to prove myself, but in an alley at the hands of a monster.* The corner of Xe's muzzle curled upwards. *Well, at least as far as monsters go, this one is nice and will probably make it quick. Couldn't ask for more in this world really.*

Kneeling, Xe ignored how cold the concrete felt against their joints. With a deep breath, they brushed their ear out of their face, raised their head and closed their eyes.

"Do you want to know my world, little one?" The arachnid's voice was close. Xe fought the urge to turn their head, to pinpoint where it was coming from.

"Do I have a choice?" The response was more of a choked laugh than anything else.

The creature laughed. "There is *always* a choice."

"I'm…" Xe took another deep breath and let it out of their nose slowly. "I'm ready."

Something brushed their face, caressing the whiskers that ran from the sides of Xe's muzzle first, then moving towards the side of their head. *He's going to bite me…*

But the sting of fangs never came.

Something like velvet wrapped around their face, and a shiver ran down Xe's spine. "A blindfold?"

The spider's chuckle seemed to echo around the rabbit. The way it moved, Xe could barely make out the sound of its multitude of joints shifting around them. Just when Xe thought they had pinpointed the creature, they would feel the briefest contact of chitin against their fur. When a leg-tip tapped the center of their back, they let out a gasp. It rested there, a heavy weight. Not painful, but a dulled spear-tip dimpling their flesh.

Then slowly it started downwards, pulling at their fur and skin lightly, not enough to hurt, but also not the most comfortable. Each agonizing inch after inch drew a noise from the lapin's muzzle, the muscles in their legs quivering. The claw reached the rabbit's lower back, then moved to the top of their upturned tail where it rested, the tip at the joining of the appendage to Xe's body.

"How does that feel?"

Xe jumped at the spider's voice, closer than they had expected, almost right next to their head. As if to emphasise the point, the claw pushed slightly, making the rabbit grunt. "I've never… I've never had someone pay attention to my tail before. I hear there are those that get off on such things, like tail-pulling or tail-brushing…"

"How does that feel… to you?" The claw circled the rabbit's tail-joint, coming to rest under it and pressing upwards.

Xe was gasping. "It feels like… by the Corporations, it feels like there is a pressure inside me, yet not the same as when I have to… damn, it feels… good."

The claw circled the rabbit's uplifted tail, sometimes pausing to apply a small amount of pressure, other times caressing the tail itself, running with the fur as the appendage was stroked. Xe tried to keep still despite their body's need to move, to beat a rhythm onto the concrete under their legs. A warning, a message, anything.

The claw came to rest under Xe's tail again, but instead of circling, it moved downwards. It caught on the edge of Xe's shorts before continuing along the tight-fitting fabric. Xe let out a gasp as they felt the hardness of the claw press against their anus before passing onward. It teased along their fabric-covered taint and finally paused, the claw pressing along the lapin's body; from anus to the smooth expanse of their crotch.

The steady upwards pressure lifted Xe slightly off the ground, using their body weight to press them against the appendage wedged between their legs. The rabbit squirmed, unable to get comfortable, yet also panting slightly.

"Your temperature is elevated, little one."

The voice had shifted position again, somewhere behind the lapin. This time they turned their head, shifting their ears slightly to try and pinpoint the arachnid. Unfortunately, the movement caused Xe's body to move, grinding the claw against their anus and taint, making the rabbit squeak.

"So you do still feel pleasure…"

"Uhhh," Xe let out a grunt and tried to move their body. "I may be sexless, but that doesn't mean… uhhh… that things don't feel good.…" A shiver passed through the rabbit and in response, the limb under them vibrated in return.

"Excellent."

"What do you me—?"

Claws moved into the grooves of Xe's elbows, bringing their limbs behind them where the same velvet-feeling fabric affixed them there. *Webbing, he's restraining my arms, and he blindfolded me…* Trying to open their eyes confirmed it. A whimper left the rabbit's muzzle. In response, the claw between their legs slowly retreated, the tip of it pressing against the smooth expanse of the rabbit's crotch, dragged across their taint, and caught ever so briefly against the indent of their pucker.

"Ugh." Xe's knees hit the pavement again, their legs shivering. They swayed for a moment, then pitched forward. Xe let out a cry and then felt the world rush upwards. Eight points of contact rested on various parts of their body and they felt like they were floating.

"Your shivers are a vibration of the divine themselves, little one. It has been too long, and my need is great."

"I will not be used!"

A claw-tip brushed the rabbit's face. "Nor will I use you, little one. I am no monster; the choice is yours. I am older than time itself, and I can give you experiences you can not believe. Grant me this gift, and I will bestow upon you your desires."

Xe sniffed the air, but could only smell the brick walls and moisture that clung to the stone. They didn't know how high they were, or if they would survive the fall. Only the eight points of contact were keeping them there, and with their arms bound they couldn't use the blade Zain had given them.

Something hard pressed against the space between their legs, a light pressure against the booty shorts the rabbit wore, the blunt tip probing their entrance. Xe let out a soft moan, the claw vibrating in response. "That's not... helping," they managed to gasp out.

"It's not supposed to."

The pressure increased, and Xe let out a squeak, their body shivering at the bolt that shivered up their spine. "Yes," the rabbit gasped. "Yes, I want it."

There was a sense of movement surrounding them, and something brushed Xe's cheek. It was ribbed, overlapping plates of something hard. It caressed up and down the rabbit's whiskers until the tip of it butted against their nose. The musky scent hit Xe hard, and the rabbit gasped. The tip of the member slipped in, just under the rabbit's buck teeth.

Xe fought the urge to gag, instead brought their tongue up

to the underside of the firmness within their muzzle. It felt like chitin, rigid, but also flexible; like a series of overlapping plates. It pressed into Xe's mouth with a light pressure, and the rabbit let it. There was a faint taste to the appendage, like smoked wood.

Just when it started to reach the limit of the rabbit's muzzle, it slowly pulled back. Xe sucked on it, pulling against the limb with pressure of their own. Their tongue moved along the underside of the limb, sliding against each plate, teasing areas where the plates overlapped. Behind them, the pressure on their anus relaxed, only to shift and move along the rabbit's taint. The pressure there soon matched the rhythm of what quickly became long strokes of the member in Xe's muzzle.

Xe moaned, and the air seemed to vibrate around them, the effect amplified in their muzzle and where a leg pressed against their taint. The smoky flavour of the appendage against their tongue grew, and a new moisture was coating the inside of the rabbit's muzzle. *It's pre...* The thought made Xe squirm, grunting as they tried the webbing that kept their limbs behind them. In response the movement of the chitinous member grew, sliding in and out of the rabbit's muzzle quicker.

I am giving head while floating... The thought brushed along Xe's mind as they concentrated on sucking on the member between their lips each time it drew back. Careful of their front teeth, the rabbit tried not to move as the spider thrust into them. Whatever fear the lapin had about the arachnid being too rough or pushing too far into their throat were unfounded. Instead the thrusts went almost to Xe's limit and then pulled back.

The vibration around them was growing in intensity, to the point Xe could almost hear it. The air felt alive, and where the spider's legs dug into them it felt like warm pulses sending waves through their body. The member in Xe's muzzle also vibrated, though at a lower intensity than the limbs holding them in the air.

Suddenly the member thrust forward. Xe drew their head back as far as it would go, sucking as hard as they could as their muzzle was suddenly flooded with thick streams of heat. Each burst landed on the back of the rabbit's tongue where they swallowed quickly.

But it wasn't enough.

With a cough the member withdrew, and Xe could feel heavy ropes of cum break as the tension between their muzzle and the appendage grew too much. Another cough, and they could hear the heavy droplets hit the ground below. Everything tasted of smoked wood and musk.

The world shifted and two of the spider's legs gripped the edge of the rabbit's booty shorts, tugging them downwards sharply. Then they hooked under the fabric of Xe's one-piece and the fabric shredded like air. Cold air chilled the rabbit's shaved body where nothing but the pink of their skin showed. It was the only way the lapin could get the fabric to lay smooth, and now they regretted it as the skin goosebumped.

A single leg caressed the bare skin of the rabbit's ass, running along it before coming to rest in the crevasse of Xe's ass. The pressure was heavy, and when it traced along the rabbit's taint, the lapin moaned. The chitin was chilled, but it only drew attention to the hardness of the shell as it ran along the yielding flesh. Xe felt their world turn again, and this time their head was angled downwards, ass in the air, a limb running along their pucker, teasing the skin.

When a hard wetness pressed against the smooth expanse of Xe's crotch they let out a cry. The limb still had some of the warmth of the lapin's muzzle to it, and it rested there, rubbing against the smooth flesh before moving upwards. The tip bumped against Xe's pucker, bringing forth a moan. Then, with a light push, the tip bumped against the opening, slowly widening it, entering the rabbit.

The rabbit's muzzle had felt amazing. The way the tongue had caressed each sensitive joint of my cock, finding every nook and cranny. There had been some concern they would have used those sharpened fangs of theirs, but I was glad I had trusted in them. The way they shivered against me, warm with heat and vibration, I wasn't able to last as long as I had wanted.

My own body rushed to climax, and I had lost myself as ropes of cum had filled the little creature's muzzle. The way they shuddered with each pulse of my own. The way when I withdrew they still tried to drink all of my gift. The way they raised their head, webbed eyes seeking me out, nose twitching, cum drenching their muzzle to hang like a forgotten web-nest.

Need flooded me. My member was hard, a rod guiding me to what I needed. I rotated the little one, my legs moving quickly. Clothing was removed or destroyed, so was the fire within my chest. The creature's shaved fur came as a shock. My claws moved from soft plushness to smooth skin, the distinction like night and day. And to feel the rabbit's smoothness where one would have a means of release was... alien.

My fascination drew me to it. I ran my legs against that smoothness, the feeling like silk of an animal sort. The creature's skin was smooth as a newborn's, not one mark or blemish to mar the perfection of the sensation. To sink my fangs into such a sculpture would be both an infinite blessing and the ultimate sin.

Instead I positioned the rabbit in a position I found agreeable and shifted my body, careful that the webbing securing me was properly anchored. I kept running my legs against the creature's body, each shiver a delicacy, each moan sending shivers along my webs to tingle along my body. My bulk came close to them, and then my member rested in the crevice of their rear.

The rabbit's body quaked, and I let out a moan of my own, the sensation causing the plates of my chitin to sing in joy. I ran the length of my cock against that fleshy mound, my tip leaving cum and saliva coating the entire length, from the base of the tail to staining the fur surrounding the shaved flesh. Shifting, I placed my tip against the pucker of the little one and rested it there.

"Please."

The rabbit's word echoed off the brick walls, and that was all I needed.

I pushed forward, slowly, letting my own cum and the rabbit's saliva ease my passage. I was not a small beast by any means, and my member was proportionate for my size. The last thing I wanted to do was to wreck the little one.

Their body resisted for a moment, then slowly their pucker opened, welcoming my girth inch by slow inch. The feel of it was astounding, the warmth of it flooding the normally neutral temperature of my body. It surrounded me slowly, enveloping me, heating me. I wanted to drive inwards, but resisted as more of me slowly entered the rabbit.

With each inch the rabbit's moans rose in volume, their body shaking. It was a delicious chorus of vibrations and sensation. The way their anus clenched and released around my shell, the way muscles bunched, clenched, released, quaked; each one a new note to the musical piece that sang throughout my body.

It was with some disappointment that I was unable to fully imbed myself within the little one, as the tip of my shaft finally hit resistance, the creature's body unwilling to let me go further. So I rested there, their tunnel pulsing against me as it adjusted to my intrusion. The rabbit let out gasps mixed with moans, their breathing fast and light.

When I started to pull back the little one's passage clasped against me, the skin pulling at my length until I was almost out. My push rewarded me with another moan, this one a long, drawn out note that rattled my webbing. Warmth again enveloped me, and I wrapped my legs around the rabbit, pulling them close. Their fur and skin rubbed against the underside of my body. My underside was my most sensitive, the location of most of my joints. The feel of the rabbit's body against those delicate sections of thin chiton made me vibrate in pleasure.

My thrusts came smoothly, in and out, each thrust bumping against the rabbit's limits. Each time I plunged into them, they let out a cry that was high pitched and needy. Their passage tugged and pulsed around me, trying to keep me within their warmth, within the comfort of their mammalian charm. There had been some concern of the ridges of my cock when I had first gone in, but now the rabbit angled their ass the best they could to rub against those ridges. The sounds they made were delicious.

I could have stayed there for eternity. I had waited too long to be with another. The fact that I had viewed this creature as food felt like a sin against the creators, against my brethren. Each thrust became heavier, harder. The rabbit was all noise out now; moans and cries shaking the webs that held us aloft. They squirmed against my underside, their fur soft to my joints, the flesh hot with heat. I drove into them again and again, my actions quicker and quicker as my need started to rise to the surface.

With a roar I came.

Burst after burst of cum flooded into the rabbit beneath me as I pushed as deep into their bowels as I dared. Under me the creature let out a cry of their own, their body shaking as if trying to tear itself apart. We stayed there, our bodies united in their dance of pleasure, the vibrations reverberating and echoing along my webs, feeding back into us. Stars danced in my mind; all I could feel was how I pulsed within the rabbit and they squeezed down on me. I revelled in the way my cum oozed its way out of the rabbit's pucker, falling thick and heavy below.

We stayed like that for ages, locked in our mating, until finally my cock retreated from the heat of my prey and into the secret area of me that lesser spiders did not own. The rabbit made mewling noises as the intruder left their ass, spasms of cum still leaking out to roll down their body. As careful as I could, I slowly lowered myself to the concrete below, cradling the rabbit against my body. I was reluctant to let them go, and yet I knew I must.

So we rested there, the rabbit against me, until finally they found the strength to lower their boots to the concrete. With deft movements, I removed the webbing from their arms and head. The first few times they blinked I marvelled at the beauty of those eyes, as best as my own limited sight could give me. Then, limbs shaking, they took a couple steps away from me before turning to face me:

A blade in its paw.

"I should kill you," Xe said, aiming the blade at the massive arachnid. Everything ached, and they were unsure if they would be able to run if they needed to. Their arm shook, making the blade dance before them. Everything seemed brighter in the alley, the glowstick long faded, yet being blindfolded had made their eyes desperate for light.

"Then do it, little one." The spider lowered itself as if bowing.

Xe paused, trying to get their body to stop shaking. The animal part of themselves wanted to kill the creature for just being that, a giant impossible-to-exist nightmare given form. They took a step forward, almost falling when they did. The spider remained in its prone stance.

"But I won't." Xe palmed the blade away. "I can't."

"Why?"

"Because you're a lot like me, I guess. People say we aren't supposed to exist in this world." Xe shrugged. "And sometimes, us monstrosities have to stick together." They turned and looked over their shoulder at the spider and grinned. "I just want to let you know... I will be back." They winked.

The spider's laugh followed the lapin as they slowly made their way back down the alleyway.

Zain couldn't believe his eyes when Xe stepped from the shadows of the alley. The Null looked like a mess; clothing hanging in tatters, dried fluids and webbing coating their fur and skin. When the rabbit saw the hyena they smiled and gave a small wave.

"You waited." The rabbit's voice was hoarse.

"You look like shit, Xe. What did you find down there?"

The rabbit glanced at the alleyway and then back at their friend. "You mean you don't know?"

"Know what?"

"Nevermind." Xe let out a sigh. "I did it. I touched the end of the alley."

Zain nodded. "I got the message not too long ago. You're in."

Xe nodded before letting out a weak laugh. "Hooray. But I could really use a long rest in a rejuvenator right now."

Zain moved over to his friend and crouched down. "Come on, get on. You look like you can barely walk." Xe climbed on without a complaint, resting their head on the hyena's shoulder.

They got about half a block before Zain turned his head slightly. "Why are you so sticky…?"

Black, White, Red

Kuroko

(CW: heavy s/m)

"Alright, you're both ready for this?" The stage manager, Gus, was a big bear, seated in one of the remote view rooms that had camera access to the stage they were on.

Vanessa nodded easily, no hitch, but Eve was slower to reply. Which made sense. If either of them had reason to hesitate, it was the bottom in this little arrangement. Especially when she was going to be handled as roughly, and for as long, as she was about to be.

Eve nodded, though, and turned to face Vanessa. The first steps of the dance were intimate but not intense. There was no dialogue called for in the script, so they made little sound as she helped strip the black and white cabbit of street clothes. A lot of contact. Neither of them was a stranger to the other, but this felt more "on" than usual. Nerves, Eve supposed. They'd been chosen for matching aesthetics, and everything else had been set up to match them. While Vanessa was a very well curved cabbit 'morph, with drooped lop ears in stark white hair, and a leopard's rosettes in white on black fur, Eve was close to the opposite. Human, slender, with pale skin and black hair. Minimal makeup, just some mascara and eyeliner.

The room was all blacks, whites, and grays, and while both of them had started in colorful street clothes, Vanessa was fully bare now, sliding into place with the room. And her transformation was only half over. Eve helped her into a black leather corset, pulled it tight, tied the bow. Plaited that long white hair and tied it with a black ribbon. Then stepped back to admire the view.

The corset had further shaped already luscious curves, and with the braid, she looked every inch the strict, sensuous dominant that she was going to play for this little video. Eve was still in jeans and a t-shirt.

Vanessa would take care of that shortly.

Indeed, after a brief moment, still and posed for the well-hidden cameras, she simply reached out and took Eve by the throat. Pushed her back, back, pushed her against the wall and held her there. Eve's hands went up, in pure reaction, grabbing at the hand clamped tight around her neck. Vanessa didn't care. She had other concerns. And Eve felt them, felt claws touch her shoulder and drag through her shirt, tearing the fabric away, and dragging hot red lines over her skin.

Eve cried out, then gasped as another drag of claws continued to rip the shirt apart. Vanessa was in no hurry, she had all the time in the world to rip that baby-blue tee to tatters. And Eve had no leverage to stop her, even if she wanted to. And she didn't, not really. She wanted to *feel* things, and she'd been told that Vanessa knew how to make her feel such intense things. This was only the beginning and she knew it. However much those little scratches hurt, and the heat they left behind, they were only faintly pink, only a preview of what was going to come later.

The hand at her throat pulled and turned, moving her a little bit to each side as Vanessa examined her work. Not satisfied, from the tsk of disapproval. Eve felt herself moved, tugged, turned around. Her back against Vanessa's pleasantly soft and curved chest. The velvet soft fur felt clean through tears in her shirt, soothing against the lingering heat of scratches. And playing such pleasant counterpoint to the first real, raw pain of the scene. Vanessa dragged claws from her shoulder, across her breast, shredding shirt and bra alike, and dragging two of those fiery lines across her nipple.

Eve couldn't help arching and crying out, squirming against

the cabbit as another drag of claws ripped more shirt, tore the center bit of her bra, and left her torso bare but for scraps of baby blue. It only took one or two tugs to rip those clear, and toss them aside. Eve didn't have to look to know her breasts, stomach, shoulders and back were crisscrossed with intersecting sets of scratch-marks. She could feel them, every one had left its sting behind.

Vanessa seemed satisfied for now, and moved on to the next stage. Rope, the only part of the scene that called for real color, a beautiful scarlet silk cord. She bound Eve's wrists together, several wraps around both together, a wrap around the middle, between her wrists, then up overhead, over a hook in the rafter. She pulled the free end down and tied it around the center cross between her wrists, as well. She paused there to take a hand at the back of Eve's neck, pull her head down and forward, and kiss the top. A motion of sensual familiarity, of comfort. She knew what steadied the human girl, what helped her endure.

And she would need it, they both knew. More rope, ankles tied wide apart, to recessed eye bolts in the floor, leaving her standing, helpless, in nothing but jeans, and panties under. Neither were going to last too much longer. And as bound as she was, she could only struggle ineffectually as she felt claws again. Bare, only the tips, each hand holding a breast, slowly squeezing, pressing claws in tighter and tighter until she gasped and whimpered. Vanessa held for a breath, then slowly relaxed her hands. Left stayed busy there, clawtips dancing over her breast, touching, dragging, drawing shapes in red lines and white fire.

The other hand slid lower. Undid the button on her fly. Unzipped the rest. Eve knew at least one camera was focused on that, and she wished, for a moment, that she could see it. Watching from outside would hurt less. But she was here, bound, feeling every tiny touch of claws. Both hands down, now, as Vanessa stayed behind her, hands low on her belly, clawtips dancing on her hips, pushing the waist of her jeans around. Obviously they couldn't go down any further on their own. That made the next step very obvious. That didn't mean it would be easy.

Denim was tougher than knit. Vanessa had to stroke her claws more than once over a line to break through, had to press harder, and the pressure rubbing through before claws made it was sensual. She could love that feeling for hours, the way she felt an intimate touch on her thighs, felt a lover's caress working to bare her, that was a sensual pleasure. One that gave her reason to moan softly, to push her hips into the hands against them, however useless that might actually be.

It shifted when those claws finally tore a long line up her right thigh. She knew in an instant that blood had been drawn, and so did Vanessa. The pained little wince and gasp, Vanessa's soft laugh, and both hands going to that tear to pull, widen it, and bare pale white flesh with a single line of red, a single drop. One claw carefully took that drop, brought it up, and rubbed it down along the length of her throat, leaving a thin smear of red there. And the first tears welling in Eve's eyes. They both knew those were coming.

More tears in her jeans, more harsh scratches on her thighs as the denim gave way, losing more and more integrity as those scratches caressed her ass, drifted up and down her thighs. Very carefully didn't touch her panties, and that careful avoidance filled her with dread. Vanessa was saving that for later. The cabbit knelt down, tugging and pulling at shredded denim, until it pooled in two piles at her ankles. She was completely exposed aside from baby-blue cotton covering her most intimate areas. She was sure it wouldn't last.

Vanessa had other concerns at the moment though. She was taking a slow walk around, at arm's length, drifting fingertips with claws retracted, stroking here or there, leaving Eve shivering with some mix of pleasure and anxiety. The slowly coiling knot of worry in the pit of her stomach as every heartbeat passed, waiting for what she knew was coming, fully aware that she had no control over when and where the next spark of pain would come.

Right breast, not claws this time. She felt the velvet soft caress, the back of a cabbit paw, the soft, cold touch of nose on her nipple, then the blossom of a dozen points of pain below, feline teeth digging in the bottom curve of her breast. She dropped her head back and cried out, tears welling again. Another bite, the other breast, a neat ring of teeth around her areola, leaving more pain, more tears. She struggled against the ropes, pulling and straining, fighting to get away from the bite. But it didn't do any good at all, there just wasn't that much give or play in her bonds.

Vanessa paused, withdrew, waited. For a moment, she let Eve steady herself. Faint caresses of smooth warm palm, and luxurious moments of velvet fur stroking, soothing. Then again, pain. Claws at her ribs, faint at first, pushing backward, up. For a moment she was breast to breast with the cabbit, feeling smooth leather, and soft fur. A moment of breathless hesitation, then a cry of pain as both hands dragged down from her shoulders, ten white-hot lines of pain as claws left trails of red behind.

She screamed, sobbed, shuddered. Vanessa held her again, waited. Head resting on top hers, Eve's face buried in soft cleavage. Under other circumstances a pleasant place. Here and now a refuge from pain that wasn't going to stop any time soon. Once she was steady again, she gave a faint little nod, a signal to keep going, and Vanessa stood back. Then the real work started. One at a time, a dozen or more precise, careful scratches, and Vanessa drew spots, rosettes just like hers, in red. One after another on thighs, back, breasts, calves, anywhere she could touch. Eve shuddered and cried, she felt the mascara streaking, new what that would look like. No one would be able to think she wasn't feeling every inch of agony.

She was very, very aware of the way it hurt, the way that continuous misery and pain were stacking up on her, weighing her down, leaving her raw. She trusted Vanessa, trusted the cabbit to know when to stop. She wasn't sure she trusted herself. And several times in the painting, Vanessa did stop, let her catch her breath, let her sobbing ebb to sniffles and shudders while she stroked soft fur over her scratches. It all ended with another slow circuit, fingertips drifting gently over all of those new spots. Even gentle brushes were enough to light the hurts back up. She knew more than a few had bled. Knew that red was all over. All over except one region, and she knew that was coming next. It couldn't stay untouched.

Vanessa paused behind her, then came in close, wrapped both arms around her, and held close, paused. The faintest of whispers, more breathed than spoken and hidden by a muzzle buried in her raven black hair. "You ready?" Eve nodded just a tiny bit. It almost certainly wouldn't show on camera, but she needed to take that tiny bit of control. She needed to be the one who said yes, even when so much of her desperately wanted to say no.

There was no reply, just hands drifting lower, one hand stopping to hold the waistband of her panties, the other going lower, cupping over her vulva, a brief pause, intimate, gentle contact, a faint little rubbing. Sensual more than sexual, they both knew this wasn't about arousal, wasn't going to end in orgasms. This was about overwhelming her with pain, until her mind stopped working for a little bit. Until the need to endure was the only thing left running.

That point was already close, and she could feel the sort of hazy cloud at the back of her mind as claws came out once more. As they dragged through flimsy cloth again. As cloth tore, and the flesh beneath lit up in bright red claw marks and intense, sharp pain. The crying started again, as claws stroked a second time, as more fabric gave way. They fell apart after the fifth pass, dropping between her feet as claws just kept going.

With nothing left to cover her, Vanessa moved faster, pushed harder, stopped giving her chances to recover. More rosettes drawn on her ass, to finish the design. So many bites, at her neck, at her thighs, at her breasts, at her stomach. More droplets of blood on claw tips and on the floor. So many tears, ugly crying and streaked mascara. So much pain. Eve lost track of everything, for a moment. Or maybe longer. That haze rolled over her and everything, for a time, was pain. Pain everywhere, her sobs and weak fighting to get away. She was exhausted, and finally, it was over.

She felt fingertips at her chin, felt a gentle kiss on her

forehead. She felt silk cords released from her ankles, then her wrists, and collapsed into Vanessa's arms. "Shh, shh... it's okay." Eve continued to sob, curling up against warm fur and leather, tight, shuddering, still hurting. Vanessa kept talking, soft reassurance, holding her tight, though she wasn't ready for words yet. The tone was important, the softness of speech even when words didn't have real meaning yet.

Eventually, Eve was able to push back the haze. Everything hurt, but she stopped crying, mostly. "Hey hey, don't wipe your eyes yet." Vanessa caught her wrist and pulled it back down. "Gotta get a couple of stills. Can you stand up for me? I'll stay right here with you. I know, I know baby, I'll stay right here." Vanessa helped her to her feet, held her while she got her balance again. It hurt to move, every stretch or twist lit the scratches back up. So by the time she was standing on her own, the tears were back in force. Not wracking, ugly sobs, but still crying while the photographer came in, while he captured dozens of still pictures of her streaked face, and all of the angry red rosettes and streaks and scratches.

When he was done, Vanessa pulled her in close again, wrapped her in a soft blanket, and just held her close, rocking and murmuring softly. Eve had no idea how long. There wasn't a clock, no outside windows in the little studio. But her looking about got an answer anyway.

"Little after four, sweet thing. Don't worry, no one's got any need to take you away. Want to get a bath and get some salve on those scratches?" Eve nodded, then shook her head. "Yes to the bath, no to the salve? Are you sure, honey?"

Eve nodded again. "If... if it's okay with you, I want to be black and white and red for a little longer. Thank you for... all of this. And thank you for staying with me."

"Aw, honey, you don't have to thank me. I'd be a terrible person if I left you like this. Come on, I'll help you to the bath, and don't you worry, I'll wash your back for you. Least I can do for the girl I just wrecked on camera. I'll tell you, honey. I could get addicted to the way you cry. It's beautiful, seeing you fall into that place where nothing matters, where all you have is reacting.

How much've you played around with that?"

"Not as much as I want. It's hard to get there, and when I am it's not like I'm the one steering."

"Oh honey, I am going to love teaching you all about it. Doesn't all have to be hurts, either. I want to see what happens when I get to play ice and hot wax over you. Paint you with shivers and fire." Everything hurt, still, but Eve smiled anyway as she kept up the conversation, staying close and leaning on the cabbit for a while longer.

The Spirits of the Wood

Nathanial LeCount Edwards

It was easy for one to offend the gods in those dark, old days. A misplaced word, an accidental gesture, even a stray thought. For no longer were the gods kind, but vengeful and full of wrath.

It was to such wrath that a young, spry buck awoke one night—warm and wrapped in the fresh, cotton sheets of his bed, his antlers cradled by a soft, downy pillow. A flash of bright lightning and the roaring burst of thunder that followed shook the house, causing the glass in the window near his bed to rattle and crack.

The buck opened his eyes and arose from the bed, the sheets clinging to his soft fur, soon draping across the floor as he approached the damaged window. Outside, he could see dark clouds covering the night sky as lightning flashed between them. In the distance, the fields that had been in his family for generations and had always produced enough food to keep the small village happily fed were being rent apart by the strong and tempestuous wind.

The buck turned and rushed downstairs, sure that he could do something to help, but was stopped by his father, sitting at the old, worn oak table by the cold hearth. The older, more worn man gestured at his son to sit next to him and the buck obeyed, sitting down on the knotted, hard bench. No words were spoken that night as the two sat there, the buck running his hands across the familiar texture of the table, and listened to the sound of rain pelting the house and the wind outside howling a mournful dirge at it stripped away their livelihood.

The next day as the bright, scorching sun shone down upon their fur, the two walked the now ruined fields. The earth had turned infertile overnight, the ground reeking of death and decay, and the puddles of water remaining were green and stagnant and horribly slimy to the touch, dripping slowly and thickly between their fingers. The father decided he would have to go to the village and ask for help. The son was to stay here and see if there was anything that could be salvaged.

As the young buck watched his father ride away on their only surviving horse, he felt a small breeze lick at the back of his neck fur, almost feeling like claws gently brushing against him. He turned with a start and saw a shimmering figure disappear into the woods at the edge of the property. Though his first instinct was to follow, he turned back and looked at the fields and buildings. Duty told him he should stay. Another breeze caressed him, and he turned to see the same figure flickered at the edge of his vision once more. He somehow knew now that it wanted him to follow, and curiosity finally got the better of him. He sprinted towards the forest, his hooves quickly taking him across the dry ground.

He soon reached the edge of the forest and stopped. Growing up, the villagers had always told him to avoid entering the ancient woods—that it was full of fey and monsters that would trick him deeper and deeper into the forest until he would never return. As he stood at the boundary between the familiar and the unknown, his hand rubbing the fresh, rough bark of a tree, the curiosity began to fade, that old, deep fear beginning to overtake it.

Before he could reconsider though, a figure stepped out from behind a nearby tree. Another soft breeze, filled with the scent of fresh wildflowers, seemed to radiate from the figure as it moved towards him. At first glance, it looked to be a lithe, nude feline walking towards him, and he wondered for a moment if he had perhaps interrupted a lovers' tryst. But then he noticed that the air around the cat seemed to shimmer, and her paws didn't touch the forest floor as she moved ever closer and closer towards him. His breath caught in his throat as he realized what it must be—one of the old fey he had heard old stories about his entire life.

Though he wanted to run, his legs wouldn't obey his mind, and as the fairy got nearer, he began to make out words whispering on the wind.

"Youngling…" the breeze whispered at him as the creature rubbed his arm, the touch reminding him of the wind whipping through his fur as he ran through the fields as a young fawn.

"Youngling," it repeated, "though you have lost the favor of the gods, they have offered you a rare opportunity to make amends."

He started to open his mouth to speak, but the voice echoed once again before he could get a word out. "Speak not, for in these woods every word is a sacred oath. But fear not, youngling, for your task is simple. You must walk through these woods blindfolded, follow the path, and attend to the three spirits that guard this land. Should you succeed, your farm will be restored to its former livelihood. But should you falter, you will become a part of this wood forever."

The buck closed his eyes for a second, contemplating his choices. But before he could open them, he felt the breeze die, the hot, stagnant air returning, moisture immediately beading on his fur at the sudden change in temperature.

On the ground in front of him, lay a white blindfold. He crouched down and picked it up. It was light as air and felt like spider silk to the touch.

He held it in his hand for a moment.

And then he put it on.

The change was immediate. Though he could no longer see, he could feel the temperature drop once again as the ethereal breeze returned. The scent of fresh earth and flowers and life assaulted his nostrils. The ground below his hooves no longer felt like dirt, but instead felt solid like stone and as he moved his foot, a loud clop echoed through the silence as he made contact. But he realized it wasn't silence. Off in the distance he could hear the sound of raging water. The only river in the area has dried up decades ago.

A shiver ran up his spine as he realized just what he had agreed to.

He took a deep breath and began to walk down the path.

He had to walk slowly without his sense of sight. Each step was a test to see if he would wander off the safety of the path. Time seemed to stretch and lose all meaning. The heat of the sun upon his skin stayed the same as he walked down the long and winding path. It could have been minutes or it could have been days, his hooves clop clop clopping as he continued forward. The only sign he was making progress was the roaring rage of the river getting louder and louder.

When the sound had grown nearly deafening and he knew he must be close to the shore, a slight smell rose above the clean scent of the water. A strong, musky scent, thick and cloying in its intensity. Even the slight whiff made the buck's head spin so much that he lost his balance, falling towards the river's sound. As his paw reached out, trying to find some purchase to save himself from certain doom, he fell into a hard torso covered in soft, silky fur.

"Well, what do we have here?" the unknown creature purred. The buck could feel the voice resonating in the chest he was pushed up against, the bass vibrating his own body like a quake. Idly, his paw traveled downward, feeling the hard muscles beneath the fur. And then his paw brushed up against what had to be a thick sheath.

He quickly tried to pull his hand away, but a thick paw grabbed his own, holding it in place, a loud, rumbling laugh coming from the beast. "I do like my worshippers when they're forward."

The buck opened his mouth to ask questions, but then stopped, remembering what the fairy had said earlier. Instead, he let the other male continue talking.

"You must be the one I was told was coming. Your task is simple," he said, rubbing the buck's held paw against the thickening shaft. The buck felt pre beginning to leak from its head, the liquid beginning to slicken up the flesh, making the movements smoother. "Pleasure me to completion, and then I'll send you onwards to the next guardian." At this, he removed his paw from the buck's.

The young buck paused for a moment. On one paw, he'd never done anything like this before— with anyone, male or female. The most he'd ever done was stroke himself off at night, hidden under his covers, trying to hide his moans so his father in the other room didn't hear. On the other paw... the thought was oddly thrilling, and he could feel his own member beginning to stir beneath his own pants. He took a deep breath and hoped the spirit would enjoy the same kind of thing he did when he pleasured himself.

He reached down once more and began to play with the still growing dick. He softly rubbed a finger across the tip, a motion that elicited a large moan from the spirit and caused a large burst of pre to shoot out. The buck quickly collected the slick, fluid coating his paws in it as he began to slowly stroke up and down the length of the now fully grown cock. At this, the spirit grabbed him and pulled him close, dragging the two to the ground. The buck landed on the spirit's chest, laying there for a moment, feeling the hard, rippling muscles full of strength and power beneath him, but he soon rolled off and continued his work. As he continued to rub at the spirit's dick, he reached down and began to play with the creature's balls as well. Its sack was full and swollen, each one the size of the buck's closed fist, and covered with a layer of downy fuzz. As the buck slowly fondled them, a finger creeping down to rub at the spirit's taint.

As he continued, he began to feel rough spikes pushing out from the shaft. From what he knew, this must be a feline of some sort. As an experiment, he lightly rubbed the now hard points and the feline let out a roar of pleasure, more pre erupting from his cock. The buck could tell that the spirit was getting close, as it's balls were pulling up, readying to release their seed, so he put his everything into stroking the shaft, the pre coating his paws doing little to ease the roughness of the spines.

The feline let out an even louder roar, one that shook the forest around them as he came. The buck felt thick cum land on his clothing, quickly soaking into it and then he felt the spirit grab him, lifting him up on his now cum-covered chest. The buck felt more globs of cum land on his back as he reached up and felt a thick, furry mane of hair.

It must be a lion, the young buck imagined, strong and powerful. Rippling, corded muscles barely contained under the golden, yellow fur the color of the sun. A thick mane surrounding his handsome, chiseled face with two deep yellow eyes looking down at him. The buck felt his own cock twitch once more at the thought.

The two lay there in silence for a moment before the Lion lifted the buck to his feet. "Very good. Very good indeed." He sounded slightly winded, and as the buck was still pushed against the feline's chest, he could feel the thick, sticky cum soaking into his clothes. The Lion chuckled, and he felt a claw push against his back. In a moment, his shirt and pants fell off him, sliced clean through by the claw. "There, much better. Your task continues though; you must go attend to my brothers deeper in the woods. Continue following the path across this bridge," at this he pushed the buck forward, and he felt the ground change from dirt to wood beneath his feet, the rushing river causing it to vibrate beneath him. "But be warned, it will only get harder from here on out." He felt two paws clasp around his ears and suddenly everything went silent. The sensation of the paws disappeared, and he reached up in panic and felt thick, smooth wax filling his ears, blocking out all sound. He reached out, trying to find the Lion, but only found thin air.

He stumbled and fell to the ground, the rough wood scraping across the skin beneath his fur, sending burning pain shooting up his legs. He felt at the wounds and a few drops of thick, sticky blood smeared across his fingers. The buck lay there for a moment, contemplating, suddenly doubting himself. In all the old tales, the fey were known for being fickle and mean. What if this was only a scheme to cause him pain?

The buck shook his head and climbed back to his feet. No, he had to believe this would work. He took a deep breath and tried to figure out how to continue. He walked across the bridge and found that there was no stony path this time. Instead, a sweet floral scent wafted up as he stepped in a bed of wildflowers. As his hooves crushed the delicate plants beneath him, he could feel the petals brushing up against his fur as the breeze carried them away.

He turned in one direction and took a step forward, only to find empty ground. He took a step back and tried another direction. In this one, the bed of flowers continued, more plants tickling his ankles. This was how he was to find his way now, a road of flowers leading him forward.

Time passed and passed as the young buck continued his trek to save the home he'd grown up at. With each step, the scent of flowers got stronger and stronger, the breeze plastering more and more petals against his skin—their silky texture soft against his fur—the heady aroma making it harder and harder to think.

Soon, he was overcome and stumbled, falling to the flower covered ground. He lay there for a moment, unable to think of anything but the scent filling his mind, his eyes under the blindfold starting to close. He was close to sleep overcoming him, the ground soft and cool beneath his bare fur. He began to stretch, hoping to get comfortable and rest his weary body when his paw brushed against something covered in rough, coarse fur.

He pulled back and quickly pulled himself into a crouching position, the shock clearing his head slightly. But before he had a chance to move further he felt the coarse fur push itself up against him once more, a strong, claw-tipped paw pushing him up against what felt like a full and round stomach. The thick layer of fat beneath the skin jiggled against him as he instinctively tried to push back against the unseen captor. Instead of releasing him though, the paw gripped him tighter, and he began to feel something hard and pointed push against his chest. Another paw grabbed him by his antlers and pushed his head downward, the unseen creature's now leaking shaft pushing against his lips. The buck remembered his previous encounter with a spirit and realized that this must be his second test. He opened his mouth and took a tentative lick, his tongue feeling the hard point at the tip of the dick, and a salty, bitter tang assailed his taste buds.

At this lick, the spirit pushed the back of the buck's head, forcing the shaft into his mouth. He choked for a second around the large cock, but the clawed paw didn't let up the pressure. After a moment, the buck figured out how to breath around it and let out another tentative lick. The response this time was a large burst of pre and the rumble of a growl shaking his body.

He barely had a moment to adjust before the spirit began to thrust in and out of his mouth, the shaft slamming against the back of his throat. The buck had no idea how he wasn't choking on the shaft, fae magic perhaps, nor did he have any idea why he was finding this sensation so erotic as he felt his own shaft once again growing out of its sheath. As the spirit continued to fuck his muzzle, the buck tried to lick at the shaft where he could and, experimenting, began to try to suck on it when he could. At one point he let out a small groan, the vibrations in his throat eliciting another growl and huge splash of pre. As he continued to attend to the spirit, he felt a thick, round protrusion begin to grow at the base of the cock.

It was obviously a knot. This spirit had to be a canine of some kind. Perhaps a wolf. The buck thought back to all the wolves in the village. They tended to be thinner, but no less predatory in their actions. However, judging by the stomach he felt earlier, this one had heft to him. Perhaps it was an older one, his fur greyed with age, but still strong underneath everything. A wolf that knew what it wanted and wasn't afraid to take him.

He licked at the knot as it entered his muzzle, and that prompted the strongest reaction from the spirit yet and he grabbed onto the back of the buck's head, his claws digging into the flesh as he thrust the shaft as deep into his mouth as it would go. The buck felt the shaft swell in his mouth and could feel the cum travelling up that shaft before it exploded into his mouth.

The buck coughed and sputtered, some of the cum going up his nose as he attempted to swallow as much as he could, the spirit's knot providing no room for it to leave his muzzle. As he felt the knotted cock pull out of his mouth, he hurriedly tried to catch his breath again, but after a moment, he realized that he was unable to breath through his nose, the previously overwhelming scent of the flowers now nonexistent. He reached up with a paw and felt at his face: first, the soft, silky smooth cloth of the blindfold given to him by the Fairy; then the soft down of his ears with the waxy lumps pushed inside of them by the Lion; and finally, the newest addition—a thick, gooey film covered and filled his nose, preventing any air from passing through.

It was then that he finally realized what the cost of each trial was—for each guardian he pleased, they removed one of his senses. For a moment, fear overtook him as he remembered the fairy's words. There had been no promise he would be able to return home, only that his father's farm would be restored. He wondered if at the end of this all, he would be reduced to nothing more than a toy for the fae to use as they pleased.

He was interrupted by his thoughts by the canine's paw placing a thick, corded rope in his paws. He felt at it—the twine was bristly and as he pulled on it, there was no give. He realized that his final task must be at the end of the length.

He shakily climbed to his feet, steadying himself using the rope and reassuring himself with the still lingering sliver of hope that he'd come out of this unscathed. Besides, there wasn't much choice left for him—he had to follow it.

This journey was the hardest yet. With so few senses left to him, the buck found himself stumbling often, scraping his skin painfully against the unusually gritty ground. But despite all his missteps, he held on tight to the rope, afraid that if he let go of it even for a second that it would disappear and he would fail.

And yet, soon, far sooner than he had expected, the buck found himself reaching the end of the rope. All of a sudden, the extremely taut rope went slack, and moments later he found himself reaching the end of it. As he held the knotted ball that signified the end in his paw, he wondered where the last spirit was.

And it didn't take long for the spirit to respond.

He felt a lithe and powerful form grip him from behind, a soft layer of fur pushing up against his back, the toned pecs and abs underneath the fur pushing up against his body for a moment. He tensed up as he felt a thick finger, slicked by something, push up against the hole of his rear, the rough appendage teasing at the rim of the opening making him wiggle against the strong arms grasping him, before forcefully slipping inside. As he tried to relax, the finger pushed up against *something* within him and he felt his own cock immediately emerge from his sheath as an arc of pleasure shot outward through his body. The finger was soon joined by another and another, and before long, the buck found himself moaning as he let loose the largest load in his life, quickly covering his own chest in hot and sticky cum.

Dizzy from the experience he'd just had, the buck barely felt when the cool and hard hoof-tipped foot pushed against the back of his knee and a quick burst of pain sent him stumbling to the ground. He crouched there for a moment, his hands scrambling in the cool, moist dirt below him, about to get up when he felt a strong hand push against his back followed by the large, warm body pushing against his own once more. Then he felt something else far different from and far larger than the earlier fingers push against his still open hole.

The buck let out a sound somewhere between a gasp and a moan as the spirit's warm, thick, cock entered him, easily pushing into his already used body. His own shaft, still sensitive from earlier let loose again, spraying the ground beneath him. He curled his fingers into the dirt beneath him digging furrows into the ground, the dew-soaked dirt soon coating his hands as the spirit began to thrust into him, his mind swirling with a newfound pleasure as the cock hammered in and out of his ass, each motion perfectly hitting whatever that spot was that made him go wild with pleasure.

As he let out another load, one of his hands in the dirt finally slipped, and he reached up trying to find something to hold onto. He found the thick, smooth antlers of another buck. He couldn't help but try to imagine the virile form of the spirit that was continuing to fuck him wild—a thin but powerful body, fur as deep as mahogany, antlers large and powerful.

And then he felt the spirit grip him harder, the pressure of its hands around his body almost painful, as it let out one final thrust before erupting into him. An addicting warmth filled his body as the young buck clenched his ass around the invading shaft, not wanting to let it go, his tongue lolling out of his mouth at the feeling of the thick cum filling him to the brim, the sensation both painful and deeply satisfying.

And then it was over. The spirit pulled out, his cum dripping down the buck's ass and legs from the overly filled hole leaving an aching emptiness within him as he felt more of the liquid coat his fur. The young buck lay bathed in their mixed fluids, the dry ground beneath him hard and reassuring against his spent body, trying to catch his breath after such an intense experience. He took a deep breath and basked in the musky smell the two had created and listened to the sound of the wind blowing through the trees.

Then he stopped.

He could smell and hear again and could feel the cloth of his clothing tight against his fur once more.

He gasped and jumped to his feet. He'd pleasured all three guardians. His task was complete.

He reached up and grabbed at the blindfold. As he touched it, it dissolved into grainy ash on his paws. The bright light of the setting sun burned his eyes after having been in the dark for so long, and he felt tears running down as fur as he tried to adjust to it.

He looked around, wondering if he'd see the spirit Buck he'd just been fucked by. Instead, he saw he was in an empty clearing, an old and decayed rope leading off into the forest. He stared in confusion for a second, remembering just how new and strong the rope felt in his paws. He followed the rope for a minute and came to another clearing. He stopped and stared. This one was filled with dead flowers, their petals dried and crisp on the ground beneath his hooves.

He followed the path of dead flowers, knowing it would lead to where he met the first guardian. The shell of a bridge crossed a dead, dried riverbed. The buck crossed the long empty bed, stirring up dust and grit. At the other end there was the remains of the path he had originally followed, covered in moss and leaves.

And then he emerged from the forest, leaving the realm of the fae behind him. In front of him, he could see his house and farm. His breath caught in his chest and he saw the fields full and fertile, gleaming golden in the setting sun. As he walked towards the figure standing in front of the fields, his father, he felt a swift breeze brush the fur of his neck from behind and the sweet scent of wildflowers tickle his nostrils, his cock momentarily tenting in his pants as he thought of his experience in the woods and the myriad men in the village.

HEARING

Blind as a Bat

Jay Coates

A mouse followed a bat up a long staircase.

Silver, named for the silver stripe that ran down his back, led the way. The bat was inky black but the for stripe of lighter fur that gave him his name. Like most of his species, he wore a sleeveless tank top, as little else accommodated his wings. A downwards-facing red arrow adorned his clothes, with the words 'THIS WAY UP' written upside down just above the base of the arrow. His long, sharp claws clicked on the concrete stairs that wound up to his apartment.

Behind the bat scurried Sierre. The grey mouse followed after Silver. Her feet beat a nervous patter on the stairs as she hurried to keep up with the larger bat. It was her first time going to Silver's apartment, and she wasn't quite sure what the bat had in store for her. All he had done was promise her a wonderful time. Right now, she wasn't having one. Her chest heaved, and her thighs burned. She had lost count how many stairs they had climbed.

"Sorry again about the lift," Silver said, glancing back at the mouse and grimacing. He scratched idly at one of his massive ears with the claw of one wingarm. "Forgot it wasn't working. I normally fly up."

"It's... fine..." Sierre panted. She was glad for the moment of rest, and she rested her hands on her thighs as she leaned over slightly. She wheezed in a couple of deep breaths. The snick of a key in a lock caught her attention. She looked up to see Silver pushing open a door into a dark room beyond.

"Come on in and rest for a bit," Silver said. He held the door open for the mouse, who cautiously stepped forward into the darkness.

Sierre got a brief look at a mostly bare floor, with a small kitchen off to one side. A doorway further inside led to another room, though to the mouse it just looked like a void of darkness. A curious lattice ran across the ceiling. That was all she got to see before the door closed behind her with a gentle click. Not a single scrap of light reached her eyes. She gasped at the total darkness and felt a gentle touch on her shoulders.

"A few steps forward," Silver said softly.

Sierre shuffled forward awkwardly. She could hear the ruffle of Silver's clothes as he followed right behind her, even as his claws left her shoulders.

"Is there any light?" she asked nervously. Her ears twitched as she strained her eyes to see anything, but there was nothing there. No light managed to creep into the apartment, not even between the cracks around the door they had just come through.

"Nothing, sorry," Silver replied. His voice was a little quieter and further away.

Sierre turned slowly on the spot and immediately lost her bearings. She could no longer remember where the door was, nor even the wall. She reached out with one hand to only grasp at air. She tried not to feel too nervous, but her heart thumped loudly in her chest as she forced herself to stay still.

THUMP THUMP THUMP

CLICK TAP CLICK

Claws tapped against glass. Running water flowed and swirled around the glass, changing in pitch as it filled. Claws grasped at the tap and the sound of water ceased. Clothes rustled and approached, and for a moment Sierre almost imagined a silhouette moving in the darkness.

"Hands out in front of you," Silver said. His voice startled Sierre, who hadn't realised the bat was so close. She did as she was instructed, and a glass of chilled water was placed in her waiting hands.

The mouse gratefully took the glass and drank from it. The icy water felt lovely after the exertion of walking all the way up to the bat's apartment. When she finished draining the glass, she realised that she could no longer hear Silver nearby. The only breathing she could hear was her own, and there was no rustle of clothing or the gentle snick of his claws as he walked.

"Silver?" she squeaked to the darkness. Her ears twitched for any sound of the bat, but she could pick up nothing at all.

The mouse took a couple of cautious steps forward. Her heart was really loud now. Blood thundered through her ears, and she could hear little else.

TAP TAP TAP

Sierre let out a little squeak of surprise. A claw tapped against wood. It didn't sound too far away.

TAP TAP taptaptap TAP TAP

The mouse turned her head back and forth, trying to work out just where the sound was coming from. "Silver, is that you?" she asked. She gripped hold of the glass in her hands tightly. She wrinkled her nose, but all she could smell was a scent neutraliser. There was no indication where the bat might be. She had only the gentle tapping to guide her.

The tapping got louder as Sierre slowly crept forward. Her steps were slow and careful as she made sure she wasn't about to kick into anything. One hand was outstretched, but away from the wall she couldn't feel anything.

Silver whistled softly. Sierre turned her head towards the sound. She adjusted her steps slightly so she walked to him. A claw touched her muzzle and she stopped. The glass was gently taken from her grip. She heard it as the glass was put down on a nearby table.

"Is this how you are normally at home?" Sierre asked. She knew bats generally had poor vision, but she had never known anyone to willingly plunge themselves into such darkness before.

Two claws touched against the mouse's muzzle. She could hear the bat breathing softly. "Always, yes."

Sierre squeaked and tried to reach out to touch the bat, but she only grasped air. "Isn't it scary, not being able to see anything?"

Silver laughed. His laughter was soft and chittering, almost like a staccato of squeaks. "I can see you just fine." His clawed wingtips moved from her muzzle to brush over her ears. Something felt a little strange about his wings, but she couldn't work out just what was amiss. "I can see you just fine using these."

"Your ears?"

Chitter-chitter sque-sque-squeak

"My ears," Silver replied, his words punctuated by his laughter. "I can hear everything. All about you. Your movement. Your heart."

Thump... thump... thump... thump-thump-thump

"I can hear it getting faster," the bat said. His wingarms moved again, pulling Sierre closer. She felt his lips against hers, and she gasped. She realised why things had felt a little odd. He was perched from the ceiling. Their muzzles locked together for a few moments. Sierre could feel the bat's smile.

The bat pulled away from Sierre. The mouse could hear his claws snick against the lattice of grips that ran across the ceiling. "Follow me," he whispered.

"How? I can't see you," Sierre replied.

Chitter-squeak-chitter.

"Follow my voice. Follow the sounds I make."

Sierre gasped and closed her eyes, for all the good that did. Her ears twitched as she heard the soft noises of Silver's claws moving against the grips on the ceiling. It was only a small sound. A gentle *sqrrk* of claw against rubber. She could hear him breathing. The rise and fall of his chest. She couldn't hear the flutter of his clothing.

The mouse took a couple of steps forward. Her feet barely made a noise against the wooden floor against the sound of her heartbeat as it roared through her twitching ears.

Silver's wings rustled as they moved. Sierre locked onto the sound and took another couple of uncertain steps.

"That's it. A few more steps that way," the bat said. He chittered softly again as he guided the mouse through the darkness. "Stop there and turn to face me again."

Sierre's ears flicked as she stopped. She strained to hear

where the bat had gone and found that the sound of his claws on the lattice came from her right now, rather than in front of her. She turned on her toes to follow the sound.

Sqrrk… sqrrk… flutter-flutter… sqrrk

The bat slowly moved further back. Sierre could hear his wings adjust against his torso as he walked back on the ceiling. His claws seemed unerring as they gripped onto the lattice above. He moved with more confidence than she did, and she was the right side up.

"Nearly there," Silver whispered. He didn't need to speak any louder. With Sierre straining her ears for every sound, she was able to hear even the quietest noise inside the apartment.

"Are you taking me to your bed?" Sierre asked. A blush warmed her cheeks, and she was glad that Silver wouldn't be able to see that particular detail.

"I don't have a bed like you do," the bat admitted. He chittered and giggled nervously.

Sierre opened her eyes and was almost surprised when she continued to see nothing. "Then where do you sleep?" she squeaked.

"Up here," Silver breathed. He whispered close to her ear again, making the mouse gasp in surprise. She hadn't heard him come so close. "Don't worry. I have a guest bed. I don't expect you to hang from the ceiling with me."

"Appreciated," Sierre giggled. She could only imagine how ridiculous she'd look if she tried to hold onto the ceiling and hang down with just her toes for grip. She would be very glad of the darkness, but she doubted the lack of light would mask the thump and crunch of her hitting the ground every few minutes.

With that mental image filling her mind, she took another couple of steps. Her elbows bumped against a door frame as she moved between two rooms. Still the *sqrrk* of Silver's claws preceded her.

"Wait there," Silver said.

Sierre stopped. She spread her arms out. She couldn't touch any walls. The floor was varnished wood, but she couldn't feel anything close by. Wings fluttered, and claws snicked against the floor as the bat came down from the ceiling. He pressed up against her.

"I didn't think I could hear your clothes," Sierre giggled. That blush warmed her cheeks again as she rested her hands against the naked torso of the bat.

"Is that a problem?" Silver replied. His nose touched against her ears.

"Only that I'm still wearing mine," the mouse responded. Her fingers gently brushed through his coarse fur until she found the leathery membrane of his wings.

A deep rumble emanated from the bat's chest. "Well, why don't I fix that?" he asked. His wings embraced her fully. He pressed her head to his chest, where she could hear his heart beating in time with hers.

"Please do," the mouse squeaked in response. She gasped and shivered as the bat's clawed wingtips teased at the collar of her shirt. Slowly, the claws softly traced down her back, before the bat pulled away from the embrace.

"Don't move," Silver said softly.

Sierre nodded instinctively despite the darkness around her. But then, she had to remind herself, Silver could still see her. It was only she who was blind without light. She listened to the bat move around her. Occasionally one of his claws would lightly touch against her fur, but otherwise he didn't seem to be doing much. He made a few chittering noises as he circled.

Chitter-squeak-chitterchitter

Sierre tried to remain still and silent. It felt like she was alone in the dark. She could see nothing and feel nothing but the clothes on her body. She couldn't even smell anything. But for the soft sounds of the bat's movements she would have been deprived of every sense she had.

The claws of the bat finally slipped in beneath her clothes. He was taking it slow—so slow that Sierre was desperate for him to speed up, but she couldn't even reliably judge where he was.

"Step forward," Silver said. He pulled down on the mouse's skirt, and she clumsily stepped out of it. Fabric rustled as the skirt was tossed to the side to land elsewhere. Her shirt followed a few moments later. Her arms raised up as it was pulled over her head, leaving her standing in just her underwear.

"I can hear your heart beating faster. Are you nervous?" Silver asked quietly. His nose lightly brushed against Sierre's right ear, and his wings enveloped around her body once more.

Sierre shook her head. "Excited," she replied. She shivered from the bat's touch, but he pulled back once more. He gave off a small squeak of approval as he vanished into the black void of senselessness. She gasped in surprise at being left alone again. "Maybe a little nervous."

"I can stop if you're not comfortable," Silver said.

Sierre's eyes tried to lock onto the bat as he moved around. She thought he was standing right in front of her, but she kept her hands down by her sides. "No. Don't stop."

"If you're sure," Silver said. This time his voice came from lower down, and Sierre gave off a little squeal of delight as she felt the bat's nose touch against her crotch. His teeth gently bit into her underwear and pulled down. His wingarms stroked through the fur on her legs. The bat's voice was slightly muffled as he spoke around her clothing. "You sound eager."

"Uh-huh," Sierre replied. She shivered, and her long tail lashed around. It thumped against the floor a couple of times.

"Never done anything like this before?" the bat asked. His voice was clear again, and her underwear was bunched up around her ankles. The mouse shook her head and squeaked as she stepped out of her underwear. She kicked them away without a thought. She braced herself for another touch to come from the bat, but nothing came.

Chitter-chitter-chitter

The bat squeaked in laughter. "Then I'm going to love hearing all the little noises you make," he said. His breath was gentle as he leaned in close. The mouse could hear him close to her chest, but she still didn't move to find him. "The noises are best, don't you think?"

"I've always liked seeing their eyes," Sierre admitted. Her cheeks burned as she admitted that.

Another little chitter of laughter. "I always liked the sounds," the bat said. A couple of claws traced softly up Sierre's belly.

The mouse gasped again. A soft moan was followed by a nervous chuckle. "The sounds are nice too," she conceded. She felt a claw slide around to her back, where it quickly and dextrously unhooked her bra. It felt to the ground to be kicked aside and forgotten about.

Sierre expected another touch to come from the bat, but he toyed with her by staying away. He didn't even say anything. Instead he just paced around her, with just the gentle click of his claws against the floor to betray his presence.

"You ready for the fun bit?" the bat eventually asked.

Sierre heard Silver jump up into the air. His wings fluttered for a moment, and his claws squeezed around the lattice grips on the ceiling with a slight clatter.

"The fun bit? You mean this isn't it?" Sierre replied. She giggled as she blindly groped forward, but she couldn't find the bat at all.

The bat slowly moved above her. Something soft rustled nearby and fell from the ceiling. "Take two steps back," Silver instructed.

Confused, Sierre did as she had been ordered. She squeaked in surprise when she felt something touch her back. Blindly groping around, she found it to be some sort of rope or harness. She stroked her hand around it. She could feel something almost like a sling with a couple of hoops in the corners. "What's this?"

"Reach up. You should find somewhere for your hands. The same for your feet too," the bat explained. He skittered around above her, and the harness stiffened slightly in her touch. "It will keep you closer to me while I'm up here."

"O-oh," the mouse gasped. She shivered in delight as she realised what it was, and how it would work. She pulled herself up onto the sling and hooked her wrists into the loops at the top. It creaked a little as her weight settled on it, but she was able to lean back slightly and keep herself suspended off the ground. She took a few moments to get comfortable. The harness was light enough that she barely felt it around her body, but it kept all the weight off her arms and allowed her to feel almost like she was floating.

"How's that?" Silver asked. He chittered close by, though his head was now below Sierre's as he suspended upside down from the ceiling.

"Perfect," Sierre replied. She tested the harness by pulling down on it slightly, but it didn't move at all. Whatever it was secured onto was strong and stable. She shivered in anticipation as she heard the bat adjusting his position in front of her, stepping across to a closer grip.

"You haven't heard anything yet," the bat replied. He giggled softly. Then he placed his wingarms on Sierre's hips. He pulled himself closer to the mouse and ran his nose between her legs. She gasped in surprise at the cool feeling of his nose, which quickly turned into a muffled squeal as his tongue flicked out to slide across her sex.

The mouse panted softly and kept her eyes closed. She tried to imagine the scene visually as she leaned forward in her harness to brush her nose against the bat's cock. She was rewarded with a few loud chitters and squeaks, as well as a slightly deeper exploration from Silver's tongue.

Breathing heavily through her nose, Sierre started to work her tongue and lips over the shaft hidden in the darkness in front of her. She trembled a little from the work Silver was doing between her legs, occasionally letting out a squeak that escaped through her nose. But that stopped after a short while as the bat swung back, moving just out of reach.

"You're quiet?" he asked with disappointment in his voice. "Are you not enjoying it?"

Sierre squeaked a little and nodded. "I am," she said quickly. A blush burned her cheeks again. "Guess I'm just used to not making much noise."

Silver chittered and moved in close again. "Well, with me, please don't hold back. No one but me can hear you in here," he said. Again, he nosed around Sierre's crotch. His muzzle and tongue explored her, and this time she tried not to hold back. She let out a few appreciative gasps and squeaks, before she remembered to lean forward and take the bat's cock into her mouth as well.

Sierre worked slowly over the shaft. At first, she had to make a conscious effort to keep making those little noises of appreciation. She made herself squeak and moan in time with the bat's tongue, but then he pushed a little deeper inside her and the squeal of pleasure was genuine and unprompted.

A low groan came from the bat between her legs. He squirmed in delight as the mouse's tongue teased down his length. His chittering squeaks were constant. He didn't seem to need to draw breath. He had no trouble in maintaining his audible responses while still pleasing Sierre with his tongue at the same time.

Chi-chi-chi-chiiii

A-ahhh, rrfff-uhhhh

Though Sierre couldn't do much with her hands, she didn't think she needed to move much at all. The two both panted and moaned at each other's tongue. Sierre's pants became more high-pitched as the bat's tongue pushed in a little deeper, exploring her faster and more frantic. They were then cut off as she took the entire length of Silver's shaft into her muzzle. She didn't stop moaning though. Her throat vibrated around the cock, and this time it was Silver's turn to slow down and pause for a high-pitched trilling moan.

"Don't stop," Silver managed to moan out between his frenzied squeaks and trills.

Sierre didn't slow down. With her eyes still squeezed closed, she let the sounds they were making wash over her ears. Her moans melded into his. She could hear their hearts beating in time.

thu-THUMP thu-THUMP thu-THUMP

Little slurps and laps filled in the gaps between the moans and squeaks. Silver was almost purring as his tongue teased over Sierre. She whimpered softly and tensed her fingers. She couldn't see his eyes, but he could feel the breathiness coming into his squeaks. She knew he wasn't going to last much longer. And nor would she.

Squeee-aaah… chi-chi-chi

Silver's wings fluttered as he wrapped them around Sierre. He pulled them both into a tight embrace. Swaddled by his leathery wings, the bat's moans and squeaks became a little more muffled to Sierre. She flicked her ears as she tried to keep focused on them, but her attention soon turned from his muzzle to what he was doing to her.

Pant-pant... ah-aaaaahhhhh...

Sierra couldn't hold back. She resisted the urge to throw her head back and cry out in bliss. She kept her lips around Silver's cock, her tongue still working over the sensitive shaft, but nothing could hold back the frenzied—if muffled—cries of pleasure.

Silver kept his muzzle buried between her legs, even as he unloaded a series of chittering squeaks from his throat. His whole head vibrated from the force of his vocalisations before he finally arched his head back and let out a single piercing shriek that just went on and on, undulating through many different pitches.

Sierre was so focused on his blissful trill that she almost didn't notice his orgasm. Her sense of hearing was so overwhelmed that her others had shut down to experience the sounds of pleasure. She swallowed and finally let her head fall back. Her tongue lolled from her mouth as she just breathed heavily. Her pants were no longer lustful and desperate. Now they were satisfied. Contented.

"Oooohhh…." Silver shivered and slowly loosened his wings. "Chi-chi-chi…."

Sierre didn't think she could bring herself to say anything. She just sighed loudly and let out a happy groan.

The mouse heard a gentle thump, and for a moment she was alarmed. It sounded like Silver had fallen from his perch, but then she felt his wingarms around her again. He had righted himself, and slowly helped her out of the harness. She dropped back down to the floor and leaned against the bat. His heart was still racing. She was sure hers was just as loud.

Sierre's legs shook as she allowed herself to be walked slowly through the darkness. Something soft bumped against her legs, and she was gently lowered down onto what felt like a perfectly ordinary mattress. She giggled into the darkness.

"Thought you didn't have a bed," she said. Her voice still sounded light and breathy to her own ears.

"I have a guest bed though," the bat replied with a giggle.

A mechanical beep chimed, and a small red light gleamed through the void. Sierre had to shield her eyes for a moment. An amber glow then began to diffuse through the room, gradually increasing in intensity until Sierre could properly see again.

"And you have lights too? Scoundrel!" Sierre lightly swatted the bat across the muzzle. He was lying on the bed next to her, a grin on his face. His eyes had lit up brightly.

"It was fun though, wasn't it?" Silver replied.

Already it was starting to feel like an intense dream. With her eyes filling in all the details around the room, nothing seemed as exciting. Being suspended in the air wasn't as fun now she could see exactly what the harness was and how it was made. And seeing all the little tail flicks and ear movements meant that the sounds Silver made just weren't as interesting.

"Very fun," Sierre said. She leaned forward and pecked a quick kiss on the bat's muzzle. "Though I think I already know what I want to do next time."

"Oh yes?" Silver asked, cocking a brow up.

Sierre stroked around Silver's massive ears. He trilled out happily from the touch. "I think we should muffle our ears and do it with just sight next time."

The bat blinked in surprise. "Mmm, well I suppose that's only fair, isn't it?" Silver said. His grin flashed wider. "Got the best one first though."

"Hah. We'll see, batty. We'll see."

"I won't hear against it."

That got the bat another swat across the nose, but the two quickly descended into laughter as Silver wrapped them up in his wings once more.

Symphonic Completion

Al Song

People always asked me why I needed to wear earbuds when I was out and about, and I would always tell them it was because of high school. Walking from one class to another was basically a nightmare. I was the only one who was out in my high school, and whenever I walked through the halls, I would hear either something homophobic or someone trying to get my attention to be rude to me.

Earbuds would be my shield against hearing something unpleasant and having that ruin my day. We can close our eyes, but we can't all close our ears, so it was always best when I could choose what my ears would be exposed to.

Sometimes the outside world sounded just completely daunting. When I took my earbuds off while riding the bus, I would just hear unpleasant conversations along with angry traffic noises, and the bus itself was a rattling tin can rolling down the highway. The world just sounded so warped and ugly in contrast to the beauty I could fill my ears with.

I always had a portable charger on me along with an MP3 player—yes, an MP3. Of course I had music on my phone, but my MP3 could hold so much more, and I didn't have to decide between my songs, pictures, or apps, and I just kept adding to my collection.

The problem with being a fruit bat is that everything we hear is amplified, and it's not difficult to listen in and eavesdrop when you're trying not to, especially when you don't want to. Being a bat also allowed me to wear my earbuds and know where people around me were since the noise they made bounced off me, and

I could tell if I needed to be on guard.

The nice thing about being a student is that I got a discount for going to see symphonies and orchestras perform, but the problem of being a student was that I knew I was going to be in a lot of debt when I graduated. There was still always that part of my mind that worried and hoped that I would make something of myself, and that I would still be able to afford to see performances.

And I was still in Seattle serving bubble tea and waffles. It was the summer before my senior year of college, and I was spending my last summer break working even though I knew it was my last chance to relax before retirement, but I felt that it was more important to have some spending money than it was to stay at home and play videogames and practice my piano and flute. At the moment I was on a bus headed toward Bellami Hall to listen to the Seattle Queer Symphony perform. Bill and Janet were going to meet me there and help me take my mind off of Francis moving.

It was a month and a half ago when my boyfriend left for Berlin to get his master's in international business. I missed Francis so much. We were together two and a half years ago when we met in a wind ensemble class. It's also where I met my closest friends, Bill and Janet.

The bus rushed across the bridge over Lake Washington, and I stared out at the scenery before me. To my left was the downtown skyline and to my right were the hulking steampunk monoliths of Gas Works Park.

I had texted Bill and Janet each to see if they had arrived yet, but neither of them had texted me back. Worry and doubt started to manifest in my stomach, since the last time this happened they stood me up, and it wasn't unlike them to cancel at the last minute.

As I got closer and closer to the venue my stomach became queasier. I then opened my phone and looked at the photos of Francis along with the two of us together. It was us at our favorite Indian restaurant, Vayu's Palace. It was also the last dinner we had together. I swiped the screen and it showed the two of us after our last performance together in the campus band class. We were performing at one of the local high schools auditoriums along with one of the community bands. I swiped it again and saw a picture of us with Bill and Janet. The two tigers smiled brightly, sandwiching us between them. The last pic I looked at was one with Francis and his oboe, except he was wasn't wearing a tux, or anything at all. I was glad no one was in the seats behind me.

Soon I got off the bus and headed toward Penniman Hall a block over. I walked around to see if Bill and Janet were around outside. Maybe they deleted the email with their ticket information from theirs phones and were in the will call line, but I didn't see them anywhere.

The doors were already open, so maybe they were inside already. I tried to find them in the lobby and noticed that there were only a few attendees in the beverage line, none of whom were Bill or Janet.

I took my seat and kept checking my phone in vain. The sunken feelings in my gut had set in when the lights dimmed and there were two empty seats flanking me.

Soon a tall fennec fox stood in front of the curtain and talked about the importance of the arts and programs that help and are inclusive of the LGBTQ community. She thanked us for attending the event and hoped that the performance would fill our hearts and minds with joy and artistic wonder.

The first piece on the pamphlet brought me back to a few years ago. Symphony no. 8 by Franz Schubert, which most people knew as the *Unfinished Symphony* was one of the main reasons why I wanted to see this performance.

I remember the first time practicing Schubert's eighth symphony. I was a flutist in the University of the Pacific Northwest's wind ensemble, and Francis played the oboe next to me. On the first day of class we were allowed to sit where we wanted within our instrumental sections, and I preferred not to have the foot joint of another flute near my head, and Francis wanted to be in the center to see the conductor better.

Francis wasn't majoring in any of the music programs, but

he always had a passion for it, and he wanted to keep up his skills and love for the oboe. He said that he fell in love with its odd timbre and that its sound just sliced through the other instruments' without needing to be loud and blaring. He said that he was already a spectacle being a large kangaroo in small-town America, and he too didn't need to be loud to be heard, so the oboe fit him well.

I picked up as many instruments I could get my paws on, but the only ones I put forth a lot of time and dedication for were the flute, guitar, and piano, since every music major needed to know piano. It was the lingua franca of Western instruments.

On that first day of class, we were sandwiched between Bill and Janet, who kept trying to talk to one another. Bill played the clarinet and Janet was a fellow flutist. I had just introduced myself to Francis and thought he'd just be another student I would only see for the rest of the quarter, and maybe someone I would have small talk with now and then, but Bill and Janet talked about how the escape room they wanted to do needed a minimum of four people and it was music-themed room. I had done a few, and it sounded exciting. Then Francis and I volunteered at the same time and we smiled at each other and the rest was history.

The four of us had so many great memories together. Together we had watched so many superhero films, learned to play various complex German board games, and attended different musical performances.

I wasn't sure what was going on with them and why they had become flakier with me over time.

Behind the curtain it sounded like they needed to tune and warm up just a little more. Then the vixen who made the announcement appeared as the curtains parted as she tapped the baton to the time and pointed at the bass section.

When I saw that she was a circular conductor, I gulped, but the rest of the strings filled in the higher ranges at the correct moment, and the oboe started its small solo with expert precision.

I closed my eyes as I let the music paint the canvas of my

mind. Images of Francis and me performing together filled my head as I heard the flutes chiming in with the melody, and soon the entire orchestra's sound swelled and erupted with so much wind and string power. Suddenly there was silence, and slowly the music gently sprouted and grew into a roar again.

It all reminded me of a time of us in a practice room late one afternoon playing the sections we had the most difficulty with as we shared the same piano bench. As we progressed through the phrases I fingered the keys with rote perfection as I tongued each note on my flute with professional precision.

The two of us reserved an hour in one of the music hall's practice rooms on a chilly Friday afternoon.

Despite focusing so much of his energy on making sure he did well in his business classes, he still made time for music. Even when he practiced with me for fun I never heard him squeak. He had so much tone control and never had issues jumping between the different octaves. I knew the flute was one of the instruments that took the most amount of air to produce a sound, but I still was unable to circular breathe, and at times I struggled going from forte to pianissimo.

Francis did say he had issues whenever there was a complex run, and he knew at times he could get a little ahead of himself and rush without realizing it. He told me that my ability to play a phrase consisting of a cluster of triplet and sixteenth notes perfectly was something he envied. He told me this as he held my paw, and of course we then kissed.

We had gone on a few dates already, but this was the first time we had been in a room alone together. I felt him open his muzzle as he lapped at the inside of mine and I opened up for him. Our tongues danced as I put a paw on his belly holding my flute in the other. He then cupped my butt cheek, and I felt a stirring in my groin.

He moaned and I parted from him. I put my flute on its stand and the tall kangaroo followed suit.

"Someone's got another woodwind," Francis said with a smirk.

"I see you've got a flute I'd love to play," I replied.

We tried stifling our giggles, but the dam busted open, and the padded room was filled with laughter.

"Ugh, what's wrong with us?" I said wiping away a tear.

"I guess another thing we have in common is that neither of us can smooth talk." He grinned at me.

"I still like your voice." I then kissed his muzzle quickly and smiled up at him.

"Yeah?" He cupped my cheek, and I nuzzled his paw.

"It's a nice area between a tenor and a bass, and it's so sweet. In my mind it's a warm golden honey."

He then put on a radio announcer voice: "Does it still sound nice when I say 'all-you-can-eat buttermilk maple syrup pancakes fresh off the griddle'?"

"Yes, it's dreamy, as the nineties English-dubbed anime girls would say." I was feeling blood rush to both my face and groin.

"Let's put on some music to help drown out what we're gonna do."

"Heh, sounds good to me," I said with a hot face. The basement practice rooms were devoid of anyone, and barely anyone booked a practice room on a Friday afternoon, but I knew precautions were a good idea. I mean I haven't heard of anyone getting expelled for having sex outside of a dorm room or apartment, but I didn't want to take the risk.

Francis played the eighth symphony on his phone and turned the volume up. He moved a small shelf with a few textbooks in front of the door since it swung inward, and he reached into his backpack for a piece of tape and a sheet of paper to cover up the little window exposing us.

The red kangaroo smiled at me, and I looked up at him grinning back. I nervously placed my paw on his flank as he reached his behind me, then under my shirt and he pulled my torso towards him. Our muzzles met, and I put both my paws onto his belly and rubbed it slowly in big circles as he moaned into me.

I then began squeezing his pecs as he lifted my polo shirt and broke our kiss but only for a moment. My breaths were heavy as I looked up at his gentle smile.

"You can go lower, if you'd like," he said in a husky tone. It was deep, raspy, and sultry, and my ears perked up.

"I'd love that. Keep talking to me." I grinned up at him.

"You like dirty talk during sex, huh?" he said moving his muzzle closer to my ear and giving it a little kiss.

"I've never actually." I looked down and clasped my paws together.

"You wanna know something?" he asked as he held my paws in his.

"Hm?"

"I haven't either."

I felt some of my fur and nerves smooth out at the sound of that.

My paw cupped his bulge with one paw and stroked his large tail with the other as I shut my eyes and felt him pull me closer. I straddled the piano bench and rested my groin against his chubby butt and thigh.

"Do you like that? You do, don't you? Feel my cock straining against the fabric. He wants to be free," he said as he grunted after voicing his desires.

"Yeah, he does. I wanna let him loose," I said as I reached down to cup his bulge.

"Nothing's stopping you, cutie. Let him be free."

I grasped the zipper and pulled it down. It was quick and sudden like a record scratching, and it made me jump in my fur with excitement.

"Oh wait, there's some more fabric in the way. I think you might need to take care of that."

I undid Francis' fly and the music the air reached a fever pitch as the brassy horns blared.

He stood up and I opened my eyes to a pitched white tent as the jeans around them fell down.

I got on my knees as he led my face into his groin as I huffed his scent. The strings from above roared as my muzzle licked and sniffed at him as he emanated such an intoxicating musk from his stiff desire.

He slipped his thumbs under the elastic of his briefs and

pulled them down as the strings amped up their bowing.

As the last note of the phrase struck, Francis' thick cock sprung up and slapped me in the muzzle. His large, heavy balls hung under a girthy member. I could see just a bit of his glans peeking through his foreskin.

"I know it's not that long," he chuckled nervously.

"But it's so thick!" I exclaimed with a grin.

I then put my lips around his needy cock and tasted some pre jetting onto my palate. He cradled the back of my head in his large paw as he guided me along his trembling length. I reached a paw under my chin to play with his hefty sack splayed on the piano bench.

My throat was eliciting moans as his head smacked against the back of my muzzle. He then moved his paws down to my shoulders and massaged them as I bobbed my head back and forth against his cock in tune with the bowing of the cellos and basses.

He smoothed my fur as he petted me and my ears reflexively went back.

I then lifted my head from the pulsing member as I pulled his foreskin back and focused my attention on his dripping head. Within me there was such a desire to please him to the fullest.

He started grunting and patted my head with a gentle firmness. "So good, but too much."

I slowed my roll and focused my lips on the engorged tip. It seemed like his was even more sensitive than mine.

"Mm, that's better, cutie," he groaned as I continued my beginner's performance. He then tickled me under my chin. "I wanna see what you've got going on down there, if that's alright with you."

I pulled back and unzipped my khakis. I pulled down my blue briefs and showed myself to him. My own cock was an inch or so longer but I was much skinnier than him. I began stroking myself allowing my head to feel some fresh air as I tugged my foreskin back and forth over it.

He reached down to stroke me with one paw and gently squeezed my balls with the other. The kangaroo then got down and placed me into his muzzle.

My hips bucked unconsciously, and I apologized but he said it was fine. He kept up with the rhythm of the piece playing atop the piano and then he placed his paws on my cheeks and squeezed them as he bobbed his head back and forth against me.

I started rubbing the top of his head along with his big floppy ears, and he looked up at me, removing my member from his muzzle in the process.

"I'm getting close," I admitted. "Can I play with yours more?"

"Of course," he said as he stood.

I lowered myself to my knees and played with his head through his foreskin, which made him elicit a few moans. These happy sounds were like music to my sensitive ears. I massaged it a bit more before showing off the big, shiny tip.

His glans received a big kiss before I started stroking him faster with a stronger grip. I also paid more attention to his big, warm nuts, which made his grunts and moans crescendo as he began thrusting his thickness in my warm muzzle.

"I'm gonna nut, Gus," he said between heavy breaths.

I just kept working his hefty nuts and bobbing my head up and down against his needy, leaky length.

"Gonna cum, gonna cum, gonna cum," he grunted in sequence as he pistoned his cock into my throat like heavy beats slamming against a bass drum.

His desire was music to my ears as I started stroking myself faster. I felt my own need and desire rising up in my tightening core as I listened to the fury of his snarling groans. My nose was pushed into his pubes as he let out a final wail overpowering the piece that played above us, and I felt him finish in my muzzle as I drank down his warm essence.

During the latter half of the first movement the piece ebbed and flowed between soft and gentle, elongated notes to short booming ones blasting in fiery succession. It was at one of these serene dips in the piece when I heard Francis whisper, "Cum for me, cutie," between exhausted breaths as he slowly rubbed my ears.

It just required a few more strokes from me, but as soon as he said that I inhaled a deep breath through my nose and cried into his groin as my muscles tensed and the entire orchestra from his phone blared. I pulled my foreskin back and blasted my pearlescent desire, feeling my muscles tense as the music, Francis' breathing, and my whines all mixed together. My seed audibly splattered on the ground as I buried my face again in the big kangaroo's pubes taking in shallow gasps of air. I was thankful the floor was tiled instead of carpeted since I could clean it with a paper towel and some water.

After that the two of us straddled the piano bench and held one another. He pulled me close and kissed me above my left brow as he played with my ears. I inhaled his sweet scent as I rested my head against his chest listening to his heavy heartbeats pounding against my temple.

Ever since that day I associated the piece with us. The oboe's cry sliced through the entire orchestra, like a siren bringing me back to my senses yet burying me deeper in my memories.

It wasn't until I opened my eyes to the sparkling theater of black and gold that I realized I had been sporting a chub as the piece played. I was definitely glad I was in the dark with no one in the seats next to me.

When we performed the piece at the end of the quarter, we only played the first two movements, and I told Francis that I wanted to write the rest of the movements, but I knew it would be a challenge that would take me a while. I was used to mostly writing songs for my acoustic guitar, and the most I practice I had at composing pieces happened during my music theory courses. Francis suggested that maybe I should try a composition class out, and I've always been grateful for his advice.

The orchestra members skillfully made their way through a couple more pieces from Debussy and Khachaturian; then we had an intermission where I bought an extremely overpriced sparkling water, but the sound of the bubbles escaping the glass bottle was always entertaining to hear.

As I drank from it and walked back to my seat I turned on my phone. I got a text message from Bill and Janet that read,

"We're sorry, we completely forgot. I lost my phone and Janet's phone ran out of power and we had to buy a whole new charger for her."

Instead of leaving me in the dust, I wished that they would've just told me that they didn't want to go with me. They could've arrived late. It's also not like there weren't any stores that sold chargers within walking distance from their apartment.

If this were the first time it had happened, then I wouldn't have minded so much, but this had been happening for a while. When Francis first left, they were there for me, but as the summer progressed along, I saw them less and less.

I only lived about forty minutes away from the university by bus, and I knew I was saving money by staying at home rather than living in a dorm since they recently renovated our dungeon-like student housing buildings into shimmering mini-penthouses.

When I finally got home, I turned on my laptop and hopped in bed. I plugged in my earbuds to the laptop and sat cross-legged in my bed. I opened up Scope and typed to Francis, "How's it going, hon?"

He then wrote back, "Doing good! Would you like me to call you?"

"Sure," I wrote back and instantly heard the nautical notes of the incoming call music. I clicked the "accept" button in the center of the screen. We did FaceTime once in a while, but I usually preferred calls since my laptop was older, and I liked focusing on my roo's voice.

After a moment of silence, Francis said, "Hey, can you hear me?"

"Yeah. Loud and clear," I replied.

"How are you doing?" It was always one of the first things he asked me. He always wanted to know how I was first, and he was definitely the more resilient one out of the two of us.

"Well, it's been an interesting day." I knew I could've been less vague, but I didn't want to throw everything going wrong with my life on top of him if he was having a bad day too.

"What happened?"

"You know me that well, huh?" I started to fidget my fingers.

"I'm your boyfriend. Of course I know when things aren't going well for you."

"It's about Bill and Janet."

"What happened?" he asked with his voice flattening.

"They stood me up... again."

"I'm sorry, hon."

"Why are they doing this?"

"I'm sure it wasn't on purpose. I mean we're their closest friends. Did they have a reason for ditching you?"

"Bill said he lost his phone, and Janet's phone was dead, and they didn't have a charger."

"Oh, yeah, that sounds...."

"Like they didn't want to hang out with me."

He went quiet.

"I'm sorry for interrupting." I then quickly shut my muzzle.

"It's okay. I know you're not feeling the best, and what they did wasn't okay. I mean they still could've gone."

"It's just so frustrating. Why do they have to keep doing this to me?"

"I don't know, but they're our friends. Let's give them the benefit of the doubt."

"Yeah, maybe," I said glumly.

"Hopefully they'll be able to make it up to you, and I can try to talk to them if you'd like me to."

"That might not be a good idea, since they'll think that I've been gossiping about them."

"Alright, hon. I'm here for you if you need anything."

"Thanks," I said with a sigh. "It does mean a lot to me. I mean, I can't really talk to anyone else about things like this. So, how was your day?"

"I've been studying so much. I don't feel like even college-level German classes could've prepared me for Germany, and all of my courses are in English. I've had so much reading to do."

"I know you can do it, hon. I mean you've taken four classes at one time before."

"Yeah, thanks, hon. How was the gay orchestra?"

"Fabulous," I said. "I got a boner when they played *Unfinished Symphony.*"

"Of course you did."

"I get one too when I listen to it. Did you jerk off in your seat?"

"No," I said quickly. "But I wanted to."

"Speaking of music that turns us on, how's composing the rest of the symphony going?"

"It's going in a really slow manner. I know I need to set up some deadlines for myself or else I won't actually end up doing it."

I always carried some blank staffed paper and a pencil. My phone had an app in which I had the necessary tools for the job, mostly the mini-piano, but I knew I did my best work for composition classes when I actually sat at my piano and focused all my attention on the blank staffs before me.

"Well, if you finish it before I go back to Seattle during winter break, then we can play it together."

"That's true."

"We can make new sexy memories with our favorite fox, Schubert."

Sound was just the ripples of molecules in the air registering through my eardrums for my brain to interpret as information, but that red kangaroo always knew how to turn those soundwaves into a fire under my tail and crotch. At times his sultry voice was enough to get me close with no other stimulation.

"Hon?" he quickly asked.

"Yeah?"

"Are you touching yourself?"

"Of course not," I replied with a grin.

"I can hear your smile through the call."

"I shouldn't have taught you the skills of how to listen like a fruit bat."

"You taught me all your secrets about your ears and what you like to hear."

I could almost feel his warm breath against my ear as he

whispered how much he loved me. "I'm very thankful I did."

"Hon, remember when we were in my apartment and we watched the video of those two dingoes going at it?"

"Yeah, and they were so buff. The one on the left was wearing a blue jockstrap and the other wore a green one."

"Then I pulled down my jeans and you cupped my bulge," he said with a moan into my ears. "You reached beneath my underwear and gave it a good squeeze."

"You were already really hard," I said as I pulled down my sweatpants.

"True, but so were you," he retorted. "I pulled you close to me and kissed your temple and whispered, 'Whose dick do you think is bigger?' What did you say next?"

"I said something like the guy on the left has to have a bigger dick since the bulge is so big, right?" At that moment I needed to let my boner free and tugged down my briefs.

"Yeah, and then they started kissing."

"And grabbing each other's crotches," I said slowly. "They were massaging their bulges, just like when I cupped your balls and fondled you." I pulled my foreskin back and forth along my length, letting it glide back and forth over my needy, sensitive tip.

"Then they got so hard and pulled down their jocks."

"The one on the right had a longer cock."

"Yeah, I was like, 'Check out his huge knot. It's as big as a tennis ball.' Then what did you say, hon?" the roo asked with a chuckle.

"The other dingo has bigger balls," I replied.

"Yeah, his giant nuts were the size of billiard balls. I wonder if he has trouble walking with those around. I mean I have no idea where you could hide them." He grunted a few times. "Then I stood up and got you to your feet. I took off your briefs and you pulled mine down. Then I started going down on you."

"I went down on you though."

"Go with it, hon."

"Okay," I said quickly as I kept massaging myself.

"Remember how good it felt when I stroked your dick and

shoved my tongue under your foreskin?"

"Ung," I replied.

"Yeah, you do," he said with a soft growl. "Then do you remember how it felt when I pulled your foreskin back and started sucking on your big cockhead, the way I played with your big balls, the way I squeezed your thick shaft?"

"Mhm," I whined in agreement.

"You were making such happy, little squeaks. Just like right now."

I didn't realize it as his voice and my rapid heartbeat were covering the noises from my own throat.

"Do you remember the bassline? It was so cheesy," he said, and I heard the music to the video playing. It was definitely schmaltzy, but that's what kept the video so memorable. The large dingo packages definitely helped me remember the stars of the video. "Then I got behind you and pushed my groin onto your big butt."

"You grabbed my dick and you started stroking me," I said. He was now getting back into what actually happened.

"Yeah, then I got you on all fours, then I lubed my cock and shoved myself into your warm, tight ass."

He sent me the "Jerker" video link. "Here it is if you want to see it again later."

Next I could hear the clattering taps of him typing on his computer, then a couple clicks of the mouse. He then struck the spacebar like a conductor banging a baton against a music stand.

The booming basses started to bow, and soon the violins joined along. He suddenly stopped the music and took a deep breath. The silky notes of his oboe sang into my ears as he played the beginning melody.

I inhaled a sharp breath, and I could've finished at that moment.

When he finished the phrase, I heard him say, "Your silence says so many different things right now. I bet I can make you cum in just a few more notes."

"Fuck." It was all I could utter.

"Yeah, you are fucked, little cutie."

He hit the space bar again. I thought he might've broken his keyboard at that. I heard the piece play again along with his grunts.

"Remember when we fucked in the practice room?" He started humming the first couple bars of the *Unfinished Symphony*.

"Yeah, hon."

"Your lips around me felt so good," he said and moaned. "I thought you were lying about being a virgin since you gave head like a champ. Your warm muzzle never disappointed me, cutie."

His breathing hastened as my ears picked up a rapid succession of small wet squishes. He was producing so much pre as his foreskin slid and slapped against his glans. His voice was threatening to push my desire off the edge.

"Hon, I'm so close," I said quickly as I pumped myself faster as I squeezed my balls with my other paw.

"Cum for me, cutie. I wanna hear you nut."

"No, you first!" I squealed.

"If you insist," he grunted. There was a moment of silence, and then he growled, moaning my name over and over again. His bed squeaked and thudded and as he hollered and I felt myself crescendo into a fever pitch as hot waves of milky ropes gushed from my cockhead, flooding my belly with a warm delight as I squeaked and moaned during our sweet cacophonic duet. I was glad my parents were visiting friends that day.

It was the last summer break I'd ever have again, and of course I was spending it working in the food industry, with the love of my life half way around the world. It wasn't the worst working at Aria Tea.

I was at my best when all I had to do was focus on drink orders, and someone else took over the register, and another employee worked the desserts. It was better here than doing fast food since my fur wasn't covered in grease at the end of the shift.

We usually played operatic music over the speakers. I'm sure that's why the place was called Aria Tea, plus the logo had a bunch of quarter and eighth notes at the bottom of a bubble tea cup instead of tapioca pearls.

Usually the people prattled on so plaintively around me. They mostly complained about school work or relationships. Blended, sugary drinks helped to drown out their qualms, but a few days after I was stood up I overheard two familiar voices from the landing above the counter.

For the last half hour I was taking care of the dishes and when I got back to the drink mixing station I heard one of the voices say, "I'm so excited for the concert!"

"It's gonna be epic," the other said, and I could feel the grimace forming on my muzzle, but I kept my composure.

"Rachel, is it cool if I take my break?"

"Go ahead, it's getting slow anyway," my manager replied. I never did picture myself with a manager younger than me, but she was a million times better at taking charge and de-escalating issues than me, and I was only two years older.

I thanked her, threw my apron on one of the hooks and walked up the stairs repurposed from old tables with the two cotton candy blue drinks.

"I've got two Skyberry Clouds," I said to the two tigers.

"Oh, Gus," Janet said with a large, nervous smile. "It's nice seeing you, again."

"Heh," Bill squeaked as he scratched the back of his head. "We didn't know you were going to be here."

"Yeah, I thought you didn't work on Thursdays." Janet then turned her gaze away from me.

"It's summer break, and I'm picking up an extra shift, since I have so much free time on my paws."

"How did you know we were up here?" she asked.

"The same reason I can tell when Todd's French horn is out of tune from the other side of the band room while everyone else is warming up."

"Were you eavesdropping on us?" Bill's brows furrowed.

"I'm sorry, but I wasn't trying to listen in on your conversation. Though it is a little hard not to when you guys are right above me."

"So how are things?" Janet asked with a wry smile.

"Not the best."

"I'm sorry to hear that," she replied.

"Can we talk about last Saturday?" I asked. "You guys stopped texting me and calling me since."

"We thought you might be mad at us so we've just been taking some time for things to cool off," Janet said.

"But even before that you guys kept cancelling on me and you barely ever texted me."

"Honestly, it feels like we've grown apart," Bill said, and Janet nodded.

What do you mean we've grown apart? You stopped hanging out with me! I thought to myself. Despite my anger I had more tact in me pulling me away from saying that.

"If you guys wanted to give me space, then why are you guys here?"

"We're picking up Rachel to go to the Seattle Country Festival," Bill said sternly.

"Why didn't you invite me?"

"Gus, you don't even like country music," Janet said quietly.

"I like Copland."

"That's different," Bill interjected.

"My break's almost over." That was a lie.

I tried to listen to Schubert on the bus ride home, but it only reminded me of the first time the four of us played that piece together, rather than that time in the practice room.

When I got home I ran to my room and called Francis.

"Hey, hon," the kangaroo said brightly.

"Do you have time to talk for a bit?"

"Gus, are you crying?" he asked as his tone dropped.

I rubbed my eyes and felt the dampness on the thin fur on my fingers. "I guess."

"What happened?"

"Bill and Janet," I said quickly.

"Oh."

"I'm so tired of this happening."

"Tired of what?" he asked.

"Well, people leaving me, since it seems like it keeps

happening." I then quickly said, "I'm sorry. I didn't mean you."

"I know," he said with a sigh. "Things like this happen. People change and so do friendships."

"But I don't want it to change."

"My best friend from high school talked to me less and less, and it was just so painful, and she never told me why she didn't want to be my friend anymore. I haven't heard anything from the tigers either, so I'm not sure how they're feeling about me either."

I looked at the wall to a picture of us smiling together at Alki beach. "Is the wind just going to blow away the happy sandcastle we've built?"

"The wind, the waves, some destruction-prone cubs...."

"Okay, I get it," I said flatly.

"Not to make light of this of this, hon, but is it truly a happy sandcastle?"

"What am I supposed to do?" I asked.

"Well, you can make new friends. I wish I could clone myself so you'd have a version of me with free time who's also in your time zone."

"Where can I find new friends?"

"You're working, maybe you can hang out with coworkers," he suggested.

"You know that never works out. Plus, they ditched me for my manager, and they're going to a concert together tonight."

"Ugh, I'm really sorry," he said gently. "What about taking a class?"

"It's a little expensive to do that."

"I know this is hard." His voice was even quieter. "I barely have any friends over here and I'm not entirely sure what I should do. I want to try to reach out and hang out with others, but I'm also trying to balance that with making sure that I'm keeping up with my classes since everything is reliant on the final. I wish I could hug you right now."

"Here I am complaining about everything when you've got it worse. I'm sorry," I said and began sobbing again. "This is why people hate me so much. I'm so self-centered. I'm the worst. I don't deserve to have a boyfriend like you."

"Gus, breathe, you're gonna be okay, just breathe."

"Okay, okay," I inhaled and exhaled. I had to remember to do this. He was here for me.

"Listen to my voice," Francis said gently, and he began humming "'O sole mio." In my mind I counted even beats to eight as I inhaled through my nose and counted to eight again as I let it all out, repeating the process over and over again as I let my lover's voice lower my heartrate and smooth over the pain in my mind. His unmistakable timbre and melodic tones tickled my eardrums as memories of him holding me as I cried into his chest flooded my mind.

He always was there for me when I needed him most, and even though he wasn't physically here, he still knew how to ease the spiraling tempest of my mind. I could feel him holding me tightly against his big belly with his strong arms. Wiping my face I felt more tears flowing through my fur as I sniffed a few times and continued listening to the low hums.

I thought I ran out of tears when he left, but I had more for Bill and Janet.

Again I was afraid. My two closest friends were gone, my boyfriend was on another continent, the rest of my friends were at home with their families, and I was alone.

We chatted a bit more, but then I heard some snoring from my earbuds. It was one in the morning in Berlin, and I hung up.

I felt my face warming up as I gritted my teeth and clenched my fists. I felt myself slump as I shoved my face into a pillow and began sobbing while also yelling.

I opened my window, and I wanted to punch through the screen and just stick my head out, but I knew I didn't how to actually get it back on the window pane correctly, so I ran downstairs, kicked on a pair of slippers, and stepped onto the porch. I huffed the clean, cool night air as much as I could. It chilled the tears in my fur as I opened my eyes to a world above me full of stars and a few clouds illuminated by the full moon highlighting their edges. The language of the wind whispered in my ears as it blew them forward.

The world around me was so still. I heard no vehicles, no sirens, and no people. It was just the air that embraced me, cooling me down, pushing around my fur and ears. I took another deep breath and let the wind guide me back into my house.

My parents were in the living room watching a sitcom about a pilot having to deal with his quirky coworkers, managers, and passengers.

"Oh, Gus, are you doing okay?" my mom asked. "Your eyes are all red."

"Not really." I switched to speaking in Laotian just to make things easier for them.

"What's going on?" My dad asked quickly.

"Sit down. We're here for you." My mom scooted over and patted the cushion between them.

"It has something to do with Bill and Janet."

"Did they do something to you?" my dad asked as he tilted his head.

"Sort of," I sighed. "They've found new people to hang out with, and I don't think they want to be my friends anymore."

"I know you're in college and you're an adult now, but you still have us," my mom said as she grasped my paw and gave it a gentle squeeze.

My dad then started to massage my left wing and shoulder. "Yeah, let's spend some quality family time together and watch TV, like we always did before."

"Thank you, guys."

After the show I hugged my parents, showered, and brushed my teeth.

I grabbed the remote for my bed, tilted it forty-five degrees, and lifted the metal fetter attachment at the foot of my bed. I had my fetters lined with cushions, and there were clips near them to keep my blanket up.

The first time I had Francis over, and we actually had sex in my bed. I started putting it up and realized that he wouldn't be able to sleep with the bed up. He then asked why I couldn't just sleep on bed when it's down, and I told him it would be like a non-chiropteran trying to sleep while standing up. I still remember the times when I'd be at a hotel and had to sleep in a bed that I couldn't angle. Whenever he stayed over, I would keep the bed parallel to the floor so he could spoon me, which was nice, but those nights would always be restless for me.

My dad let me borrow the car to pick Francis up at the airport. I took a ticket from the machine and drove up the ancient swirling ramps to the fourth floor of the parking lot. I wandered up and down the factory-esque baggage claim area and felt a tight squeeze around my waist from behind.

"Gus!" he shouted, lifting me up and spinning me around.

We kissed in the middle of the crowded thoroughfare and kept our lips locked as we made our way to the parking lot payment machine and through the bumper-to-bumper traffic. He nuzzled me as we drove through the security checkpoint and all the way back to my house.

I was glad my parents gave us a few days to be alone during winter break as they stayed at my uncle's home. I spent most of my summer with them and getting reacquainted with distant relatives and the Lao community in Seattle. Soon enough fall quarter started again and I saw my old friends again.

After we got in the garage and out of my car, our muzzles were locked to one another's. We managed to strip as he rolled his tongue against mine. I unbuttoned his flannel and he unzipped my hoodie. He felt up my wings and butt as my paws roamed around his belly and chest.

"It's finished," I gasped after pulling back.

"You came already?" he asked with wide eyes and a grin. "I didn't know I was that good."

"No, the symphony," I said as I pointed at the piano, which had a thick binder on it.

"I'm gonna grab my oboe."

"Not if I grab it first," I said cupping his package.

"Get your flute," he said as he walked back to the garage.

"You don't think I was prepared for this?" I asked as I lifted the piano's fall and my flute rested atop the keys.

"I get it. I'll hurry."

I undid my jeans and removed my underwear and when he got back he held his oboe in one paw and the case in the other, blocking his package from view.

"You cock tease."

He flicked it open, placed it on the coffee table, and took out an oboe reed. "Open up, cutie."

I followed his order and he placed it in my muzzle. I let it soak in my mouth as he groped my crotch. He jerked it a few times as he stroked himself, and I was at my zenith. He put his fingers on my foreskin and massaged my tip with it, and I started leaking as little spurts of pre pumped from me.

After a bit he plucked the reed from my muzzle, planted it into the staple of his oboe, and played a string of notes that vibrated and bounced against my face. I closed my eyes and felt the shape of my lover and his instrument in my mind. His silhouette reached forth and grabbed me by the cock and tugged me to the piano.

I pulled out the third movement, the Scherzo, and played the melody of the missing parts of the movement on the piano keys. Then I counted us down as we sight-read our respective parts.

It was magical to be able to play with him again. I was always in a state of flow when we ran through a piece together and now we were running through something I created. It was even better having a boner and being naked with him as we played.

After we made it to the end he said, "I see you've put more of an emphasis on the flute and oboe parts."

"I wonder why that is."

"Well, I hope the rest of it is balanced."

I grinned and said, "I did let the viola parts shine in the limelight more than the violin section."

"Ah, my lover, the troll master."

"Someone has to take them down a peg, or four."

"Hey, uh, can we go to your bed?" he asked looking at the stairs. "I've been wanting to try something out for a while now."

"Sure," I said as we put our instruments on their stands and we headed to my bedroom. He dragged my mattress to the center of the room.

"Get in bed." He leered at me as I hopped onto my sheets and began lying down.

He fettered my ankles and turned out the lamp on my nightstand. The *Unfinished Symphony* started playing on his phone, and I heard a quiet motor as he lifted the bed. As the notes bounced off him and struck me, I closed my eyes and felt his form flexing in the dark as he sauntered over to me, grasping his cock and stroking it back and forth. I could feel the music showing off his foreskin covering and exposing his thick glans as he chuckled at my squeaks of delight.

I then felt his warm muzzle on my right thigh as he kissed his way down and I felt his cock against my cheek as I reached out to guide it into my muzzle. I used the other to work his hefty sack as he kissed mine and began licking and sucking at my nuts.

He popped the head of my cock into his muzzle and began humming to the oboe part of the symphony. I then felt him thrust into my muzzle as he swirled his tongue against my sensitive tip. Instinctively I squealed and squirmed, but it seemed to have fueled his lust as he thrusted harder when the music played crescendos and blared sforzandos. It was like the piece was face-fucking me as it blew me at the same time.

Soon I tasted copious amounts of pre leaking from my lover's cock and the kangaroo started making erratic thrusts. He stopped humming and started growling and grunting. With one final shove he spilled his love inside my muzzle and moaned into my groin.

The vibrations all around me created a chord that struck perfectly with my fundamental frequency of pleasure as it created an impeccable picture in my mind of what my lover looked like in the dark, and within my roo's muzzle as all my taut heartstrings were plucked in succession I achieved a harmonic progression towards completion.

TASTE

Titillating Trivia

Linnea "LiteralGrill" Capps

A bell choir composed of bottles clinking against glasses rang in the night's festivities. With a few drinks, watching Tod Turner's Tricky Trivia was quite fun. The strange facts the show presented combined with their yelling out guesses at the television had become a welcome Friday night tradition for Walter and his old college roommates.

Recently, Walter had even convinced his friends to download the show's phone app so they could answer the questions with some stakes. The person who got the least right buying the snacks for next week and the winner choosing just what they had to buy. Kade, a red panda that loved a good crunch in his food, had won the previous week. He wanted to enjoy the crunchy goodness of a 'fried food fiesta'. Zayden, who had lost the week prior, delivered in spades.

The hare had surveyed the impressive collection of cheese curds, fried pickles, onion rings, and fried okra but had ultimately chosen the simple classic: french fries. The grease slicked the white tips of his otherwise black paws as he grabbed a bite, greedily stuffing a pawful into his maw. He savored the salty starch with every crunch.

He noticed a glass being wiggled just within sight. Kade considered himself an amateur bartender and always insisted on mixing drinks for everyone to enjoy. As Walter embraced the icy glass offered to him in his paw, Kade released a sigh.

"You know I'd really love to mix you an *actual* drink sometime!"

Walter refused to let the red panda's teasing get to him as he sipped his usual: a John Daly. Zesty iced tea played against the sweet tang of lemonade strongly enough to cover the spicy brine of the vodka across his palate. Walter knew with a rabbit's stronger sense of taste that a drink with far more alcohol would be too harsh for him to swallow.

"My drink has a name doesn't it? It's just as real as whatever you're drinking!"

Kade finished the Sazerac he was mixing, playfully rolling his eyes at the hare. "Hey it's your loss man."

Zayden flopped down on the worn leather couch, wiggling as only a ferret could to get comfortable in its fluff. He reached for his thick rimmed glasses in his pocket placing them on his long muzzle so he could properly see the screen. "Come on the show's gonna start soon and I'm *not* buying next week!"

"Fine!" Kade sat down on the other end of the couch, sandwiching Walter in the middle. "Phones out lads, may the feasting and cerebral straining begin!"

Walter chuckled at the joke, wiping the grease off his paws on his jeans before reaching into a pocket to grab his phone and fired up the app.

The show began as always, the playful jingle playing before the show's host, a slim white tail deer, strutted onto the stage dressed in a snazzy vest and shirt combo and a signature polkadot bowtie. "Guys, gals, and non-binary pals, guess what it's time for?"

"Tod Turner's Tricky Trivia!" Walter joined in with the audience in the studio, punctuating the line while raising his glass. His friends gave an appreciative chuckle as Tod Turner went on to introduce the three contestants in his low booming voice.

"Now it's time for our first question! In the first episodes of the classic television show *Rickety Road*, Omar the Ornery was not green! What was his original color?"

Walter took another sip of his drink, the subtle burn of the vodka diminishing as his intoxication increased. He hadn't the faintest idea of the answer but he figured he had a one in four shot between orange, blue, yellow, and pink. He gently pressed a paw pad to yellow and enjoyed the citrus of his drink for luck.

"And the answer is… Orange!"

Walter saw the ferret lean his head back with a groan as Kade pumped a jubilant paw into the air. "Hah! Years of being raised on public television finally paid off. Score one for me!"

The questions continued and the fried foods found their ways down the trio's maws fairly quickly. They unleashed uproarious laughter upon learning that Q-Tips were originally called Baby Gays and expressed envy of horses as they learned they cannot vomit.

Walter placed one empty glass next to another, giving in during a commercial break to Kade making him what he called a Painkiller. Walter was unsure about the name, but the orange coconut bliss coating his tongue and filling his chest with warmth was hard to argue with.

The show had gotten to its halfway point where the trivia quickly became much more difficult but gave double the points. The pleasant buzzing in his head made him care very little that the dot of a lowercase 'i' was called a tittle or whatever other questions came on screen. He quickly fell behind in points, resigning himself to buy next week's snacks but fully enjoying himself.

"Now we've all heard of kissing butt, but what if it could actually be a bit more pleasant?" the host paused, allowing the audience to be drawn in. "The censors made us phrase this one really carefully believe me, but it was just too fascinating not to include! Which species has anal secretions that can be used in cherry, raspberry, and vanilla food flavorings?"

Walter was too tipsy to realize his triumphant cry at the confidence he had in his answer would bring such attention from his friends. He casually entered it in, careful to keep his phone safe from the prying eyes of Kade and Zayden.

"The correct answer is… Beavers! Oohhh seems none of our guests got that one correct! Stay tuned as after this commercial break we'll explain this fun fact before going into the final round!"

Walter had been so pleased with himself getting the answer right, it took him a moment to notice his two friends were staring at him from both sides. "Dude... How'd you know that so easy?"

"Hmm?" Walter turned to Kade, incapable of quite grasping the line of interrogation.

The ferret beside him quickly joined in. "Seriously man, nobody on the show even got it right, how'd you just know it like that?"

Realization broke through the spirit induced haze that clouded his mind. His face burned, his black ears that usually stood tall folding back in embarrassment. "Nothing... Just uh, read it somewhere once..."

He was quickly jolted from his embarrassment as Zayden clapped him on the back with a firm paw. "Oh no, no way. You're not mumbling your way out of this! There's a story here and I know it!"

"Guys..." Walter wasn't ashamed of how he had come to learn the curious fact, but he wasn't often the one to open up on something quite so sensitive.

"Oh come on Walter! Look, screw the points. You tell us how you actually knew that and I'll buy next week!"

The hare saw Kade's jovial grin and the determined sincerity in his eyes. Walter normally would have waved them off, too self-conscious to consider telling them anything. Tonight however, he was emboldened by consuming liquor far stronger than he was used to.

"Fine... Seriously though, if you two judge or tease the deal is off!"

The ferret and red panda both looked at each other, eyes slightly wide that their usually timid friend was willing to speak up. "Dude, on my honor, Kade Whitehouse offers his solemn vow that no judgement may take place in my household as this story is told!"

"Yeah but a light hearted ribbing he won't promise!"

"Zayden!" Kade took the paw he had been holding over his heart during his overdramatic speech and used it to smack the ferret gently on the back of his head. "Okay fine, minimal teasing too I promise."

Walter took a deep breath, trying to focus enough to figure out where to begin. Eventually the silence grew awkward, and he gave up, finally blurting out "I tried licking on a beaver there once myself okay?"

Two sets of jaws dropped on either side of him, his friends stunned at the answer. Walter would rarely talk about taking someone out on a date. The few times he had there was never a mention of bedding the lady in question.

Zayden regained composure first, reaching for the remote to turn down the television so they wouldn't be interrupted. "Okay we promised no being judgy, well, Kade did, but I'll stick by it too. Who's the lucky lady?"

Walter sat down his drink, fiddling rapidly with the digits of his handpaws. His nose began to rapidly twitch, a telltale sign of nervousness in the hare. "Not... Not a lady. I um, wanted to try... You know. The other, at least once. If that makes sense?"

The nerves were so apparent in Walter's voice that Kade instantly reached around his shoulders to wrap him in a warm embrace. "Dude there's nothing wrong with exploring. Hell, I've watched some videos of that and wondered now and then too."

"Wait, you really have dude?"

Kade eyed down Zayden. "Hey this isn't my turn to story tell tonight, but yeah. Got a problem with that?"

"Oh, come on! Not at all! I go to pride with my younger brother every year, you know that!" The ferret gently reached out a paw to mess up the fur on Walter's head after his response, giving the hare an encouraging smile.

"See man? There's no judgement here. Now come on tell the story!"

Walter may have been giving the warmest smile that had even spread across his maw in his life. His ears perking up and tail twitching, he was revitalized to continue his tale. He set the scene, allowing his friends to be drawn into the events from his own point of view.

It could just be one hookup right? One guy, it didn't need to even be someone he knew or would ever see again. Just a hookup to experiment a little and see if he'd like it.

The simple explanation he was trying to repeat in his head had done nothing to calm him. He tried a different angle for reassurance, reminding himself that he had been fantasizing about this scenario for quite a while. He knew that he seriously enjoyed the physique of the women he had dated. Still, the crush he had hidden on the high school star quarterback Barret Young had never left his mind.

He knew it was every stereotype come to life, but he had always wondered what it might be like if the beaver and he had been alone in the locker room. Those strong muscles, his confidence, what would he have done if given the chance?

While Barret had happily married his highschool sweetheart, there was still a chance for the rabbit to try and see this fantasy somewhat play out. He had nervously downloaded Mrowlr, knowing it was mostly used for gay hookups, before proceeding to make himself a profile. On his preferred species he only had put down beaver, hoping he would get the match he was looking for.

It had taken a week, long enough that Walter hadn't recognized the kind of notification was showing on his phone, before he got a match. He had almost opened the message right in the middle of his office with coworkers around. Flustered at the faux pas almost committed, he had excused himself into the bathroom before checking the message.

"Hey there, got a thing for beavers huh? I gotta say, I love the little white tips on your paws. I bet they'd show off so nice against your black fur when they're wrapped around... something."

The message had caused Walter's heart to jump. He could picture it in his mind, his soft paw pads gliding over the beaver's sheath, slickening as they reached to touch his long warm...

The bathroom door opening loudly had quickly snapped him out of his fantasy. He went to stand, noticing just how far out his pants seemed to be tented by his own member, before resigning himself to sit down to calm himself. He decided to take a look at the beaver's profile.

His name was listed as Anthony. Glancing over his profile picture showed his sleek umber fur and what looked to be a cocky grin that showed off the cute buck teeth his species was known for. He scanned down his athletic physique, eyes quickly becoming glued on Anthony's thick tail. His jaw dropped, noticing three piercings near the tip with eyelets showing the full tunnels left open by stretching them up in size. He wanted to read his full profile but knew he didn't have the time before heading back to work.

This was his last chance to back out. He surprised himself not taking it, overcoming his faint-hearted nature. "I'm glad you like my look! I've gotta say, I love the piercings on your tail! Plus I think I agree that could be a nice look for my paws or other parts of me."

His heart raced in his chest. He had never felt so bold to come onto someone in his life, but Anthony's charm and good looks had taken him off guard. He rushed back to his desk, eager to finish the final hour of his work day so he could safely message his potential hookup more.

He had felt a vibration that signalled Anthony must have answered from his pocket. However, he remained responsible even as the final hour of his day seemed to drag on far longer than any hour of his life had before. The moment he had clocked out his phone was out of his pocket as he practically hopped out of the building. "Thanks man! They took a lot of work but I'm really proud of them! You got piercings anywhere? Heck, what kinda hobbies you got?"

The smile hadn't left Walter's maw the entire way home despite dealing with a crowded public bus. He had gotten to learn so much about Anthony. How he worked in the IT department of a large law firm, his love of motorcycles, and how they both shared a love of ukulele music. His digits flew across his screen, answering questions about himself and sending his own questions back all with flirtatious comments in between. Walter became so engrossed in the conversation he managed to miss his stop, being forced to walk an extra mile back to his apartment.

He found himself too excited to be bothered by the inconvenience. By the time he arrived at the door he was more focused on his phone than fishing the keys out of his pocket. When his paw had finally gotten wrapped around his keychain, he instantly dropped it in surprise from the message he read.

"You know it's a great day out, lots of sun and a cool breeze. I was thinking of taking out my hog for a ride. Wanna join me? You could ride in back. I got a helmet that'll work with those ears of yours."

The small tickling that began in his stomach erupted through his entire body. His footpaw rapidly thumped against the sidewalk keeping a steady rhythm of his anxiety. Wasn't this going really fast? That cocky grin, he wanted to see it in person. Couldn't this be dangerous going off with someone he had only met online? He imagined how it would feel, his arms wrapped around Anthony's waist, leaning against his muscular back for support as they cruised the city streets.

Thoughts of what would happen if someone he knew spotted him were quickly erased by thoughts of what Anthony's wind kissed fur might smell like against the distinct scent of motor oil. Nerves quickly morphed into excitement. He decided if ever there was a moment to start being spontaneous it was now.

"A ride sounds like fun!"

"Well you can maybe have one after we spin around town of course! Where do you live? If you got a jacket you should get it on while I head there. It's good protection from gravel and things like that."

Walter hadn't missed the double entendre. He decided Anthony's boldness must somehow be infectious as he typed in his address, ending his message with a winky face. He unlocked the door and dashed into the house, hunting down the one denim jacket he owned buried deep in a hallway closet.

Walter's ears twitched, hearing what sounded like two honks outside. Was that Anthony? Did motorcycles even have horns? The roar of a revving engine quickly answered his questions. He knew the sounds were summoning him outside.

He tentatively opened the front door to reveal the brash beaver casually leaning the bike as he held its entire weight on a single leg. Sunglasses, a faux leather jacket with combat boots to match, all on a bike black as coal with accents of chrome shining in the sun. It was every biker stereotype Walter knew while being exactly what he had secretly hoped for. Over the rumble of the idling engine the beaver belted, "Hey, you coming or not?"

Walter smiled, hopping out of the door with such enthusiasm he forgot to even lock it. Anthony's voice had been much lower than he had been picturing in his head. As he approached the bike, Anthony slapped his wide tail behind him to indicate where Walter should sit. "Yo just a sec before you climb on." Walter watched fascinated as the beaver lifted up a small section of the seat, the perfect size for his tail to slip underneath before letting the section drop back down. "Custom made so my tail won't be stuck in your face!"

Walter wanted to say that he might not have minded being in those circumstances but felt more bashful with Anthony there in person. He slowly lifted a leg, attempting and succeeding albeit awkwardly to mount the bike.

Anthony handed the hare a helmet before gently knocking on the one he donned himself. Walter understood the signal, placing the helmet on his head, careful to be sure his ears would fit properly in their designated holes.

The beaver looked back, tilting his head as if to ask a question. Walter deduced he was making sure the hare was ready to ride, so he grabbed onto the beaver's waist before nodding. He could practically feel the grin on Anthony's face through his body language alone as the beaver gripped both paws onto the handlebars. With another fierce growl of the engine the riding partners sprang forward onto the road ahead.

Walter had never ridden a bike like this before but the nonchalant beaver at its helm made him felt safety alongside the thrill. Wind whipping through Walter's ears cut slightly through the engine's roar as the beaver confidently navigated through the town. Anthony avoided any traffic, his knowledge of the city streets allowing him to plan a smooth ride on the fly.

Walter was elated. Cruising down alleyways he had never seen before, enjoying graffiti murals that covered the walls, coming across buildings and businesses he had never known even existed. It was all such a thrilling adventure to him, he had failed to notice Anthony hadn't taken a turn to bring him home. Instead, he had pulled onto a street that led to the older part of town as dusk settled. Street lights flicked on, casting shadows against the brick buildings that lined the streets.

The hare noticed that Anthony was slowing down, stopping before a building that looked like it had once housed a store of some kind but had been renovated to have a small garage and living space. The resounding thunder of the engine the hare had become so accustomed to died down as Anthony turned off his bike.

"Crap… Man I'm sorry. I'm in such a habit of coming back to my place when I ride I totally forgot I had to get you home! You wanna just crash at my place tonight? I'll totally get if you'd rather head back home; I'll gladly take you back."

The pieces of the puzzle all slid together at once. That clever beaver, he had planned this all along! It was the perfect chance to get him alone. He knew Mrowlr was mostly for hookups but did all guys come on this strong? Was he even safe going into the beaver's home?

He thought it over a brief moment, trying to use logic to calm his nerves. Anthony had offered him a ride home and honestly had seemed like a quality person during their texting session before. He'd just shown him around the city with the only intention of Walter having a good time. He just wanted to keep that good time going right?

He heard Anthony chuckle. "Do you always tap your footpaw like that when you're nervous? I can't lie it's adorable. Come on. If you stay the night there's no pressure for anything else okay?"

Walter huffed, the beaver had quite easily read his mind. It had just turned to wondering if he'd be having an even happier ending to the night. This was like a dream come true, his chance to try a new experience had fallen perfectly into his paws. Despite this, he could only manage to stutter, nerves getting the best of him.

Anthony's chuckle made the hare's heart leap. "Fuck you're cute. Alright my legs are tired anyways. Do what bunnies do and hop off this bike so I can park it in the garage and get us set to go inside okay?"

Bunny? Walter had never been called that since he was a child! The name got under his skin but instead of the annoyance he expected to feel, a fire had sparked to life within him.

He hopped off the bike without comment, easily catching the cocksure grin on Anthony's face as with the click of a button a garage door creaked to life. He removed his tail from the compartment before he too hopped off the bike. His powerful legs allowed him to push it inside the now open door with ease.

"Come on, gotta get in the house through here!"

Walter realized he had been staring at the beaver's legs and snapped himself back to reality. He quickly padded into the garage before the door began to close behind him.

"I know it's a weird place," Anthony commented as he opened another door into his main living space. "My Dad owns a lot of property and thought nothing could really be done with this place so he sold it to me for nothing! I think I did alright with it though don't you?"

Walter had followed through the door to see that Anthony had decorated well. A white metal cabinet with hints of rust stood out against the russet hues and autumnal browns of the exposed bricks. The hare assumed the red logo painted on the front must have been from a vintage motorcycle company as were many of the other decorations adorning the walls. He saw what looked like a glass display counter near a corner that had to have been there when the building was a shop.

Walter turned to Anthony earnestly telling him, "I absolutely love it!"

The beaver's tail cheerily slapped the hardwood floor. "Hell yeah! I'm not some biking junky honest I swear! I just can't get enough of these old metal signs and parts. My grandad used to work on these things when they were new ya know?"

Anthony's passionate response bled into the hare's emotions. He began asking him about everything he had put on display while the beaver invited him to sit down on his overworn couch. Walter couldn't help but prod into a hole in that couch with a single digit as Anthony casually slipped out of his jacket, tossing it onto the floor. "You want something to drink?"

Walter could only nod, the white tank top that had been underneath the jacket clung tightly to the beaver's chest. It was all the hare could focus on at that given moment.

Anthony padded off to the kitchen, soon returning with two classic glass bottles of cola. He snapped the caps off deftly with a bottle opener letting them clatter to the ground before handing a bottle to the hare.

"To cute bunnies!"

There was that word again! Walter felt flustered but joined in taking a drink as the beaver did trying to hide it. The bubbly cola fizzed down his mouth and throat, sweet caffeinated goodness a delight on the palate.

He took another sip before noticing he was being admired by the beaver from across the couch. He tried to play it casual, but could feel his black fluffy tail twitch as Anthony's eyes glanced in its direction.

"Look, I'm sometimes bad at being subtle so let me just be honest. I've got a thing for bunnies and you're honestly gorgeous. Thought so the moment I saw your picture. Then you were actually fun talking to? I figured a miracle had happened!"

Walter felt too flummoxed to even reply. How could a guy as hot as Anthony be interested in an everyday bunny—darn he was even saying it in his head now, like him?

Before he could attempt a stuttery reply, the beaver continued. "I saw your profile is new, is this your first time on an app like this? You know what people usually use it for right?"

Walter was floored. He knew in the back of his mind that being invited in like this was going to lead to a proposition but it hadn't occurred to him just how jittery it would make him feel. "I um, w-well yeah. Though I've ah, um…"

"You're doing the footpaw thing again." A smile spread across the beaver's maw as Walter consciously tried to stop himself. "Spit it out, we both met on a hookup app and you're here right? What, you got some weird kink or something? I'm down to try anything out there once."

Walter spluttered, "N-No it's nothing like that! It's just um… I've never… Been with another guy before…"

Walter's voice trailed off as the beaver's eyes grew wide. "Wait so this is your first time on a hookup app and you decided to try it with a guy?"

Walter sheepishly nodded, expecting ridicule before Anthony began to chuckle. "Dude you've got balls! I mean, literally but still. Not many guys would be that brave!"

"Wait really?" Walter's ears lifted up, amazed that a beaver he assumed to be so utterly confident would compliment him on his bravery.

"Damn straight! Look, I saw you only listed beavers. You got some guy you always had a thing for?"

Walter's jaw could have hit the floor. "How did you…"

"Just putting two and two together. Listen I'll make you a deal. You really want to try this, we can go slow. Talk the whole time to make sure you're comfortable. Just promise me if it turns out this isn't your thing you won't just bail on me forever okay? Today was honestly fun…"

The beaver was finally showing a bit of his own shyness, the moment of honesty making Walter feel even more comfortable. "I wholeheartedly agree, this was too cool to just be a one-time hang out, even if things get a little spicy tonight."

"If?" Walter noticed the beaver had moved closer to him on the couch, setting his bottle on a table in front of them. "Mr. Bunny, unless you tell me no, there's no ifs or ands to this, but there might be some butts…"

Anthony reached out a paw to gently caress one of Walter's ears. Walter was unable to stifle a small sound as a spark of pleasure crackled through his body at the touch.

"You just tell me if anything is too much for you okay? I'll totally stop, you don't gotta feel guilty."

Walter nodded, but before he could say that he understood he found Anthony's lips pressed against his own. The beaver gently pulled away, moving to nibble over the small of the rabbit's neck, paws exploring their way down his waist.

Tingling pleasure crackled through Walter's body, causing it to relax to the beaver's every touch. He barely had cared that his belt was being undone, too distracted by the beaver's eager attentions, until he felt said beaver's paws wrap around his shaft.

Walter jumped, tensing slightly until the gentle pressure of Anthony's soft paws milking away at his length returned him to relaxation. The hare relished the sensation, gasping loudly. Still, he longed for more, wanting to feel a slick length within his own paws.

His breath hitched, biting back a moan as Anthony rotated a digit over his tip. "C-Can I um ah… Yours too?"

Anthony paused for a brief moment, a thought passing through his mind. "You know what a sixty-nine is?"

Walter had eagerly gotten into position, laying himself flat on the couch. He had hungrily eyed the obvious bulge in Anthony's pants, before he slipped them out to reveal his cock in its fully glory.

"G-Going commando huh?"

The beaver chuckled. "Like what you see?"

Walter was too frazzled to do much more than nod. Anthony took the lead. "I'm gonna crawl up on top of you okay?"

Walter once again nodded, the beaver moving to straddle his hips above the hare's head. The rabbit breathed in deep, savoring the woody smell of the beaver's fur, the slightest hint of musk from the member dangling above him.

He knew what he needed to do, but Anthony beat him to it. The beaver caressed the rabbit's orbs in a paw, giving his arousal that was standing at attention a teasing lick.

Walter shivered, wetting his lips. He began to lick the beaver's balls with an eager tongue, trying to give some of the fantastic sensations he was receiving. He tasted what could only be described as a gym locker room with a dash of sweat. The masculine taste made him eager for more, moving to suck on the beaver's tip, tasting the salty drops of pre that had begun to pool there.

Anthony began to swirl his own tongue around the rabbit's tip, licking just over the slit of his opening until the hare's legs began to quiver. Walter could hear Anthony sloppily sucking on his length, could feel the pleasant pressure of the beaver's maw, could smell...

Wait, was that raspberry? Cherry? Vanilla? He tilted his maw up, still keeping the beaver's length between his soft lips. He gazed up at the underside of Anthony's tail, almost certain he had caught the scent from the hole underneath. There was no way it could be coming from there of all places right? An overwhelming temptation to bury his muzzle and tongue into the tender flesh crashed over Walter. What was he thinking? It's his first time, didn't he want to take things slow?

Before he could overthink it, his paws had replaced his maw around Anthony's warm shaft. He was certain his strokes were clumsy with it being his first time in such a position, but the beaver didn't seem to mind. If anything the strong twitches he felt against his paw let him know just how much the beaver was enjoying this.

With his now free maw, he gently nosed his way under the beaver's thick tail, lapping away at the beaver's hole. Anthony clenched in surprise but didn't stop Walter from delving in further. He was met with the taste of warm flesh but was that... Cherry? Vanilla? His nose really hadn't failed him! He wasn't sure if he was imagining it but the pleasured moans he felt vibrating around his cock urged him on. His wet tongue teased over the warm flesh, swirling around the opening.

Walter could hear Anthony panting over his cock, each warm breath washing over it causing his length to twitch. "Fuck bunny don't stop, please..."

The new pet name alongside Anthony's pleading gave him a dizzying urge to continue taking his paws to grasp firmly on the beaver's rump so his maw could get in deeper. Kissing over the rapidly clenching hole, savoring the twist of fruity vanilla with every breath and lick.

He was startled as he felt his belly becoming coated in the beaver's warmth, shot after shot of the thick goodness soaking into the hare's fur. Musk combined with the sweet scents in his muzzle, the beaver's scent intoxicating to the hare.

Blood started buzzing between his ears. His partner's orgasm had ignited a carnal wick within his body. Anthony sensed the excitement, engulfing the entire rabbit's length in wet heat. It spasmed in the tight recesses of the beaver's throat, warmth firing through his abdomen, pressure building, desperately needing to burest!

Walter coated Anthony's throat with cum, his body quaking as pleasure rocketed through him. He allowed his head to lie back, tongue lolling out of his maw as his partner eagerly slurped up every last drop.

The beaver pulled up, gasping desperately for air. Regaining his composure, he lookd down past the hare's belly and his own and cracked his cocky grin. "That good, huh, bunny?"

Walter giggled, the post-coital bliss leaving him too giddy for a regular response. "Yes... Your bunny really liked it!"

"Oh it's *my* bunny now is it? Oh I like the sound of that..."

Kade broke the silence that filled the room. "So, was it just a one and done kind of thing?"

Walter looked over at Kade with a nervous grin. "Funny enough he actually kept messaging me after. We've been going on a few normal dates since then, but I was too scared to tell you guys."

"Man there is no way that if you're still seeing this guy he isn't coming over next Friday night. Tell him he gets any food he wants, it's on Kade anyways!"

Kade stuck his tongue out at the ferret but quickly nodded in agreement. "If you really like this guy, I honestly wanna meet him. I promise we'll be nice and not rip on him too hard just for you!"

Walter was about to agree before a realization washed over him. "Wait, there is *no* way he *ever* gets to know I told you this story. We got that?"

Kane belted out a laugh, Zayden quickly joining in with a giggling fit of his own. "Oh come on guys I was serious! I don't want to mess this up!"

After the two had caught their breaths, they jokingly said they couldn't make any promises on that one despite reassurances that Walter would 'owe them one'. Still as Walter left Kade's apartment that evening he couldn't help but smile, pulling out his phone to give Anthony a call.

Walter's nerves flared upon hearing the beaver say hello and ask why he was calling at such a late hour. He tried to bolster the courage he had found earlier, but the liquid that caused it seemed to be losing its effects on him. "Say um, I know we've only been going out a few weeks now... I um... uh..."

"Gosh you're cute when you stutter. It's okay, what do you want to say?"

The familiar low tones of Anthony's voice through the phone quickly calmed him. "My friends really want to meet you. You know how I hang out with them every Friday night? They agreed to get you any food you wanted if you'd tag along."

There was a pause on the other end. Walter was beginning to grow nervous before Anthony responded, "I thought you were nervous on introducing me, how did you tell them about us?"

Heat rushed into the hare's cheeks. He wanted to tell a lie but knew being honest was the right thing to do. "Well you might not believe this, but the trivia show? They asked a question that led to me telling them a very interesting story..."

Tasteful Education

Patrick D. Lambert

"This is a stupid idea..."

"C'mon Terry, it's a brilliant idea."

He couldn't contain his smile. The crocodile woke up that morning and explained his plan to his boyfriend, saying it was the right time to set it in motion. He didn't put on any clothes beside his boxers—not that he needed them in that building. Tall, and more chubby than bulky, Jay jumped like a child not wanting to step on the cracks in the sidewalk. Despite his weight, he did it gracefully, waving his arms to the rhythm of the music playing in his head.

The crocodile jumped over the center table in the common room and looked at his "fraternity brothers," the bunch of losers, weirdos and queers who didn't make it or show interest in the more serious, "actual" fraternities.

"Gentlemen! I am, as some of you might know, a big slut," he announced proudly, one hand on his chest and the other up in the air, giving him an overly dramatic air.

"Tell us something we don't know!" exclaimed the senior bull, who everyone was already missing despite it still being eight months till he graduated.

"Some even found their way to this paradise, thanks to me," he continued, giving emphasis to those last words as he glanced at the bull, who groped his bulge in reply. "Which is why I never show shame nor discretion about my busy sexual agenda. It is a social duty for people like me, born with a natural talent, to offer his services without delay and having no concern for the physical appearance, sizes or shapes. Because..."

"All males deserve to blow his load!" chanted the entire room in one single voice, much to the crocodile's delight.

"That is correct, my lovely sunflowers!" he exclaimed joyfully and proud of them. The wood under his paws creaked— then succumbed to his weight, bringing down the crocodile and a burst of laughs from the misfits.

"Well done, dumb fuck."

"Don't blame me for being this thick," he regained his composure and resumed, making sure to run his hands over his thighs. "Now, just because I take cocks on a daily basis doesn't mean I don't have standards. Sure, I don't mind what I got in my ass, but before that, I need to take a good taste of who's gonna breed me," he bit down on his lip, his words now coming out almost as a moan. "A male flavor is unique, special in its own way. You can lick a male from head to toe and know his entire story. And his cock? Oh dear me... one should make love to a cock with his mouth, lick it clean and drink his seed; I can't imagine a better pleasure than being on my knees, memorizing the unique shapes as I suck and lick and nibble."

"To the point, Little Chief!" someone yelled, despite all being captive in the monologue.

"Oh, shush!" The crocodile cleared his throat. He did resemble the look and passion of a professor. "I'm obviously worried about the lack of understanding from this simple concept. You all just want to shove it balls deep and blow your load all over the place, and you bottoms can't think of anything but being a walking fleshlight for the first stud that crosses your path! No, no, no, where's the passion in that? Where's the love? The dedication? The intimacy between two horny males?" With open arms, he turned to look at everyone with genuine worry in his eyes. "That's why I'm offering you a special class dedicated to those who still don't know how to truly...*taste* the moment. I'm waiting for you all in the locker rooms at midnight."

All he found were skeptical looks. His possum boyfriend, who was occupied with taking notes and analyzing the damaged table, raised his eyes and shrugged.

"Plus, the coach owes me a favor, so you motherfuckers

better keep your mouths shut or the entire football team are gonna kick the living shit out of us!" The sudden burst of anger took them by surprise, as if they never expected to see that face from the crocodile. He just cleared his throat and smiled back at them. "I'll be waiting for you."

The crocodile retired, followed closely by the possum.

"Jay...explain to me again why we are doing this?" the small marsupial glanced back at the group of seven that were now seeing what remained of the poker table. "You know we're gonna have to pay for a new table right?"

"I'll get a new one," he stopped in front of Terry and chuckled. "Remember how Dad's always saying I'm a failure?"

"Yeah. You pester me once per week because of it."

"Well, I was thinking I might not be good at what he wants me to be!"

"Huh, what a revelation."

"So I thought—and taking into consideration how extremely good I am at bending over—that I can be a counsellor!"

A moment of silence. His boyfriend waited, expecting the punchline or his apology for the bad joke. But none of those things happened. No, Jay continued smiling. Slowly, he put down his hoodie, now trying to place in different orders the words that came from his maw, unsuccessfully.

"Oh god, you can't be serious." Terry took a step backward and showed actual concern at the proud face in the crocodile's face.

"No, no, no, listen to me. Remember the party at Jessie's place this summer? When she started crying in the pool and made it all awkward for everyone?" Terry nodded. "Well, the next morning I made her a coffee and talked with her. I know she's a bitch, but I couldn't help but feel sorry for her, and she told me her boyfriend wasn't helping her finish like before."

"Oh, jeez, I know how much you hate those guys too..."

"I know, right? So I listened to her, discovered they got stuck in a routine, gave some advice, and look at them now! They went from 'breaking up at Starbucks' to 'We'll have three cute children in the suburbs.'"

"Oh, I didn't imagine things were that bad between them."

"Because I helped!" he sort of sang that phrase, pointing at his chest with his thumbs. "So I was thinking about that, and maybe I'm good at giving advice to other people. After all, intimacy is a very, very important thing in a relationship, and you can't deny having bedroom problems can severely affect a relationship."

"Not a problem for me, but I get the point. So you wanna see if you're good at...teaching them? You want to counsel them?"

Jay nodded enthusiastically.

"Honey, I don't think you're approaching this correctly."

"Oh, c'mon! I really need your help on this one! Look, I did my research, and sex therapy is an actual thing! Just not that common like other kinds of therapies, but still a valid one."

"And I'm sure your father is gonna agree to paying for you to get a career in that."

"No need for it. I'll start as a marriage counselor, study on my own, and pay for it myself later. It's a perfect plan! Please, just let me at least try it and see if I'm good at it."

Terry wasn't fully convinced. Jay wasn't dumb, just too...relaxed, if that was the right word. He loved him for his generosity and compassion, and knew how much he liked to help everyone. But he never saw the negative effects of his plans.

He tried to imitate the whimpering expression commonly used by canines, and while he was nowhere close to it, it still had effect over the possum.

"I'll make sure no one bothers you for half an hour," he sighed. "But you owe me a dinner after this."

"Make it an hour, and I'll take you wherever you want!"

He took the possum in his arms and lifted him from the ground, kissing him with passion. The taste of apple juice invaded the crocodile's maw.

"I'll tell the coach."

And without saying another word, the big reptile rushed towards the building's exit, leaving his boyfriend so he could think of a good excuse in case his scheme failed, which was always likely to happen.

In any other case, a scenario of this nature would have never been possible. But Jay had one hell of a tongue. Somehow, he discovered a familiar face in a popular webcam site, and gathered the courage to reach him; the coach didn't admit it at first, but the crocodile gained his trust through some...dedicated work— apparently, having an audience was a massive thing for the polar bear.

So, they made a deal. An audience in return for his help.

Of course, the deal sounded better in his head. Coach Rogers felt powerless and weak in front of the small group gathered in front of him, sitting in the now dry floor of the showers. They acted normally, talking like they did before the professor entered the room. As if watching other people fuck was nothing weird or new to them.

The coach had dreamed of this fantasy for quite a long time, and now that it was in his reach, all he wanted was to run back to his house and pretend he had never talked with Jay.

But as soon as he pictured the crocodile in his head, Jay walked in, dressed in nothing but a lab coat and his thick-framed glasses. He was smiling like a kid in Christmas who had found the biggest box ever under the tree.

The cheers from the group followed him as he approached the coach.

"Glad you could make it, sir," he started. There was no lust or desire in the gator's eyes, unlike their previous encounters. He even looked...more mature? Well, the coach wouldn't call him that, but he did have a different appearance than before.

"T-thanks..." the words came as a whisper, but Jay apparently didn't listen to him.

"Now, I'm happy to see all of you made it. Oh boy, this is so exciting! As you recall from our previous chat, I'm heavily worried about the lack of interest some of you show over foreplay. I know you're young and you probably don't think of foreplay as something important when dealing with a one-night stand. Totally understandable, no need to share that kind of intimacy with a complete stranger. But I think you can have a much better time if you take a moment to explore the body of your partner. In today's lesson, Coach Rogers is gonna help me with this task. I'll start with a favorite topic of mine," he made a small pause for suspense, "flavor. As you probably know, my boyfriend isn't as interested in sex as I am. That doesn't mean we can't have our own type of fun more focused on foreplay than penetration. He likes being licked all over, and we have found different ways to make it more enjoyable, although I must admit his natural flavor is just so irresistible," and he licked his lips to emphasize it. "As instructed, Coach Rogers didn't take a shower today. Yes, yes, some of you might don't like that, and that's respectable. What we'll be doing next depends also on your own preferences. So talk with your partner about it to make it more comfortable for both of you."

Jay cleared his throat and turned to face the polar bear, whose confused face made him chuckle.

"Coach, would you mind taking off your clothes? Don't worry, this is a safe place. My class here knows how to keep a secret."

Of course, the coach didn't believe it. There was something comical about a tall, beefy polar bear being intimidated by a bunch of horny brats, who clearly had been day-dreaming a lot about him. Well, he was sure more than one student had their fair amount of fantasies of him, and the idea of it always boosted his ego. But this was the real thing, an actual group who were about to see their fantasy turn into reality. He exposed himself with a feeling of shame looming over his head, and an erection growing as he revealed the snow-white fur covering his body.

"My, my, I did not expect a reaction this fast. You do enjoy being watched, coach," Jay praised, giving only the right amount of attention to the throbbing shaft before looking back up.

The "students" weren't that discrete. They drooled and licked their lips at the sight of the eight inches now fully hard. It surely went over their expectations.

"Now, class, pay attention from now on. I'm a firm believer of the 'show, don't tell' rule."

Before the bear could assimilate all of what was happening, Jay surprised him with a kiss. It was the first time the crocodile kissed him, and he was well received by the bear's maw. The taste of bitter beer and cheap cigarettes wasn't among his favorites, but it made him imagine the coach in his living room or in a rocking chair during sunset, beer in hand and the cigarette burning as he took another drag at it. Wearing just a tank top and his boxers, he enjoyed his vacations alone at home. Kids were playing outside, and they paid no attention to him; teenagers listened to music in their rooms, and didn't see a reason to look outside the window. He wasn't alone at all, yet he felt in total peace and confident that no one would look at him.

What a powerful image. It started to pull his shaft out of his slit. The rancid taste of the smoke, still lingering on his palate and tongue, became more tolerable, even pleasant, mixed with his saliva. The crocodile trembled, wanting to taste even more of it, thinking how exciting it would be to hold in his lips the same cigarette the coach had smoked.

Before he could think of anything else, Jay moved apart from the bear's maw and went down his neck.

"You see... most people prefer to wash their fangs before kissing," he resumed his class, talking between licks in the sensitive skin. "It's respectable and understandable... but sometimes it's ok to just... jump right into the other person lips and, if you're ok with it, enjoy the taste of it. Take your time to identify each one of them."

Salty, but not too much. The fur wasn't as thick as he expected, and his long, serpentine tongue moved freely across it, dragging the sweat with it. The cheap cologne tasted odd, like something spicy. And when he closed his fangs, just pressing so softly at the skin, it sent a shock throughout his spine. The coach moaned, not used to that sort of feeling and sensation, and all the people looking at them just made it more intense.

"Why is taste important...? It tells you a lot about...about the other person," he raised one of the bear's arms and shoved his maw in his pit. It was saltier there, mixed with the mint flavor from his deodorant; the last one wasn't too strong, and it was the smell of it who helped him to perceive it. Depending on how long it had been since they applied it, it decided how creamy it felt. The coach used it early, probably thinking his smell was too bad for him. "Mr. Rogers here... he likes to smell like mint, a good option to cover the musk, but can be bad for some sensitive tongues."

He continued despite that. The coach spent a lot of time outside, under the sun. His sweat was a sign of a long day of work and effort, and he loved that in a man. Just bathing in his musk wasn't enough for him; Jay praised that smell and taste. It was all about their virility. And the crocodile wanted to carry it with him.

His tongue moved from the pit to his chest, where the taste wasn't that intense. His tongue followed the trace left by the drops of sweat that rolled down his chest and belly, like the one left by ants to mark the route to find food. He knelt in front of him, but ignored the hard cock resting over his shoulder—while the smell was alluring, it was the part he always left for last.

Instead, he snapped his fingers, and Terry appeared inside the showers with a cheap plastic chair. He placed it behind the bear and instructed him in a whisper to sit down. He did so. Terry smiled to the group and left to keep looking for anyone that might come too close to the locker rooms.

"As I said, you can know a lot about someone by just tasting his body. Routines, habits, the type of care they put in their fur, all kind of stuff," he cleaned his maw with the back of his hand. "Of course, it also depends on your own limits. It's no good to force yourself to endure certain flavors that might not be of your liking. This, for example," he took the bear's paw and raised him to match his maw. "Disgusting for ones, enjoyable for others, paws can have a potent taste and smell according to their hygiene habits. I do ask for a certain standard, because even I have my limits."

He placed his nose against the sole. It was so warm. The smell didn't differ a lot from their pits; maybe a little stronger. The taste was different, thought. The rough texture from the sole felt weird against the slick and smooth tongue, a sensation he never got used to. And it tasted sour. A bit of talcum here, a bit of dirt there; the more he licked, the more it made him think of a spoonful of any sort of powder.

"Of course, coach is a clean male." The bear giggled a bit as he said that. "The taste of his paws is more or less similar to how my own paws taste after a day outside." Another giggle. "Nothing too disgusting, if you're used to it." And another one. "This is a flavor you can get used to—would you cut that out?!" he commanded, moving his paws apart and looking at the coach.

"S-sorry, it tickles."

"Well you certainly won't be my assistant for the next class. But yes, that is also a thing you should take in mind. Tongue textures differ among species, and it can affect how others react to your licking. Also keep in mind how sensitive they are, and adapt yourself to it. If they don't like licking, try bites! Some even might find it more exciting than a wet tongue, and if you want to roleplay it's also highly recommended to try biting. Just be careful."

Jay continued with slower licks, taking his time to enjoy the salty flavor. Of course it wasn't the best, but he focused on making his tongue motions visible for the rest of the group, hoping to be a good example on how to do it. But the coach continued giggling, and it distracted the crocodile.

"Well, this isn't helping," Jay sighed. "However, exploration is highly recommended to understand what your partner likes. Some even find tickles enjoyable; you might never know until you try it. A good tongue can do a better job than five fingers."

No need to keep the class waiting. He knew they weren't that interested in what he was saying, but more in the coach and his throbbing cock. His erection didn't lose any firmness, not with so many people looking at it. Jay had already felt that shaft deep inside his ass and slit, and while the bear knew how to give a good fuck, the crocodile opted for a more...oral treatment. After all, the shape and length were perfect.

Some cocks are too small. Some others are too big. Their thickness also plays a major role. You can work around that, it depends on the tongue and skill. But some cocks were naturally perfect to give a good blowjob.

Its smell was magnificent, but he wasn't a particularly musky bear. Jay wanted to taste it. Holding the shaft from the base, he closed his lips around the head and started moving his tongue in a circular pattern, taking with it every drip of pre that came out. The bear moaned, and his body trembled in the chair. The amusement from his group didn't hold back, and "wows" and "damns" were heard the more he sucked on the delicious cock.

Sweaty, salty, and at the same time, sweet. Not the bitter taste from the first time, but a sweet flavor; not too strong, just enough to notice it. The coach listened to his advice, after all, and Jay couldn't be happier—after all, what you eat affects your entire body, even the taste of your cum.

One hand over his head, and the entire length went inside his maw and deep into his throat. His flavor was perfect. The soft texture of the warm skin against his palate made him smile, the cock throbbing as pre went right into his throat. He pictured the coach in the field, walking barefoot over the wet grass, giving indications to the team and getting them ready for the next game. He runs from one side to the other, following his boys. His sheath is all sweaty now. His thighs and balls too. He fans air at himself with his hand, before cleaning the sweat from his forehead. He wants the training to end...

...because when it does, he waits for his team to go into the showers, to clean themselves and joke about their days. And while they do that, the bear takes a random jockstrap to sniff at it. He sits there to jack off while they're at the other side, unaware of what's happening. Jay can taste the water-based lubricant he uses, mint-flavored like his deodorant. He knew he used a lot: his entire cock tasted like it, even the sheath. It makes the blowjob easier and better, as Jay knows there's not much more time till the coach exploded. But that's what made it better, right?

The coach started to hump faster at him, no longer feeling shame. It was the same rhythm he jerked off with. Fast and steady, not leaving a single part unattended. It was stronger now, the taste of pre on Jay's tongue. The coach leaked a lot when he was excited. And when he smelled a used jockstrap it probably was very exciting; or maybe it was the sensation of the thick fabric against his tongue, if he dared to lick it—Jay knew he would.

"Fucking hell..." the bear muttered, his orgasm too close to prevent it at that point.

Good, he didn't want to stop. Jay felt every throb from his cock. Jay bet the lubricant wasn't enough for the bear when he jerked off by himself, and that the bear probably spat on his cock or used the jockstrap to finish off. Dirty, soggy, and now covered in precum. What a delicious combination. How exciting would it be to use a jockstrap that someone else used as his cumrag...

And before he could picture that, the bear flooded his maw and throat with his orgasm. Holding him against his crotch, the crocodile swallowed as fast as he could. The sweetest cum he had ever tasted, a mixture of juicy fruits turned into a substance that he drank devotedly. What a warm sensation it left on its way down his belly, thick enough for him to feel it sliding through his gullet. And he wanted more of it. All of it. He sucked and licked to get every drop of it. His tongue played with the cum, too good to swallow it all.

The sensitive bear pulled out his cock, whimpering from the intense climax he just reached. His fantasy, now complete, and wanting to bask even further in it.

The crocodile, hard as rock and with cum dripping from the sides of his maw, took a moment to regain his breath. Such a good, strong flavor was too good to keep it for himself; before the coach could regain his strength, Jay stood up and rewarded the bear with a taste of his own seed, kissing him with passion as the class awed at his audacity. Whether he accepted the liquid because he wanted it or out of surprise, Jay didn't care. He drank it, and that's what mattered for the crocodile. After pulling apart from his lips, a thin rope of cum mixed with saliva remained, connecting both maws, only to break when the crocodile turned to face his class.

"As you can see, proper foreplay can make the orgasm even stronger," he managed between huffs. "Of course, we don't have enough time to go through an entire session. But I'll be more than... happy to answer your doubts in private. As for you, coach," he stood up and glanced at the bear, thinking of all the places his tongue didn't reach during his class. Jay leaned down to whisper just for him. "I think you'll be happy to know that you're today's homework."

"What?"

"It is important for you to explore your own limits, guys." He was facing his class again, ignoring the confusion in the bear's face. "Take a partner and lick him all over. If this is new for you, go for someone you trust, it makes it easier. If you have a better notion of what you can endure, the coach will be happy to help you go even further."

"What?! Wait a minute, this wasn't part of our deal!" he exclaimed, now feeling betrayal and a growing desire to beat the crap out of the crocodile.

"I'm pretty sure jerking off to your students' musky jockstraps wasn't part of your employment benefits either, but I see no reason to remove that from your contract—or you, from the payroll," Jay muttered just for him, making sure the coach listened to him through the cheers of the groups. "After all, you'll be happy to know you have a fan among your team—who told me about you—, and he's super eager to take a private lesson with you. What kind of teacher would deprive a devoted student of his desire for knowledge? I think you should take this as practice."

Jay left, and his students moved apart to make him way, all of them staring viciously at the polar bear. Drooling fangs, throbbing bulges, a strong scent from various men mixed together. The coach took a step back but was quickly surrounded by the group, who held him from wrists and ankles and held him down. In mere seconds there was no sight of the bear, only a bunch of horny guys growling and huffing as they licked every part of his body, not caring at all about the smell or taste. The coach laughed at first from the ones licking his paws, but his pleasure came back quickly; his own fantasy was surpassed, never expecting to be praised like that. The crocodile might have gone too far, but he'd find a way to get him back. His erection returned slowly, and he let out a loud moan as two long tongues fought over who would suck him off. He was too tired to fight, and too excited to stop them. Knowing there was nothing else he could do, the bear opened his legs for the class to lick every part of him.

Jay smiled, looking at the scene from the threshold of the showers. Terry approached from behind, whistling at the show.

"So you found a perfume to rule over the world," he acknowledged.

"What?"

"Never mind, I'll tell you later." He took the crocodile's hand. "I'm happy you found yourself. I believe you'll be a great therapist in the future."

"Oh, thank you. That's kind of you, hun."

"Don't take me wrong. I always believe in you. Just try to plan carefully next time instead of doing the first thing that crosses your mind."

"Really? Even if that's licking whipped cream from your back?"

"Huh... well, I think we can make some exceptions," he chuckled, and stood over his toes to kiss Jay on the cheek. "I'm starving; why don't we look for something to dinner? Assuming you're not full yet," Terry cleaned some cum from the side of his maw, but before he moved away his hand, Jay took it to lick the white topping from his index.

"Hun, you know I always have room for more."

BIOS

Linnea "LiteralGrill" Capps is a three time August Derleth award winning poet and award nominated author. She's also a smoking hot grill on the internet constantly getting up to shenanigans and out exploring the world. When not seeking out adventures and experiences, she happily plays songs on her ukulele and writes the stories she dreams up every night before bed. You can find information on her other works at **www.linneacapps.com**

Alleged human who would much rather be a stoat on the internet (so long as he can still have his cup of tea), **Jay Coates** lives in Australia, where he spends most of his time complaining about the heat and trying to write the many stories stuck inside his head. He has a particular passion for non-human characters, and will write as many of those as possible.

Kyell Gold has won twelve Ursa Major awards and a Coyotl Award for his stories and novels, and his acclaimed novel "Out of Position" co-won the Rainbow Award for Best Gay Novel of 2009. He helped create RAWR, the first residential furry writing workshop, and has instructed at each of its sessions through 2019.

He lives in California, loves to travel and dine out with his partners (when possible), and can be seen at furry conventions around the world (when possible). More information about him and his books is available at **http://www.kyellgold.com**, and you can follow him on Twitter at @KyellGold.

Joel Kreissman is an underemployed biologist from the frozen wastes of Wisconsin who tries to put his degree to some use in his science-fiction writing. He posts his stories to FA and SoFurry under the handle of "Zarpaulus" and has a novel and a short story collection published.

Hi! I'm **Patrick D. Lambert.** Half-time crocodile and creator of tales of horror and debauchery—sometimes in the same story. That doesn't mean I don't enjoy making a touching and lovely romance or, in this case, a messy ode to the flavor one can just enjoy in the preamble of sex. If my work in this anthology isn't enough to satiate your instincts, you can also find other stories in *Breeds: Wolves* or *12 Days of Yiffmas*. And you can always contact me on Twitter @ProfeLambert.

Al Song is a Laotian-American red kangaroo living near the caffeine-fueled city of Seattle. He has majored in German Studies and Comparative Literature, and he plans to one day use his degrees to go back in time to interview Franz Kafka. When the roo isn't writing or working, his guilty pleasures include watching competition reality shows, wasting time on viral videos, figuring his way out of escape rooms, thinking up how to parody top 40 music on his guitar, and playing flirty bards in tabletop role-playing games. Al has also been published in Fang Volume 8, Roar Volume 9, The Furry Cookbook, Tales from the Guild 2: World Tour, and Foxers or Beariefs. He will also be published in the upcoming anthologies Howloween Vol. 1 and Difursity.

You can find more of his scribbles at **furaffinity.net/user/alsong**

Weasel is a queer, biracial author and The Dude of Weasel Press. He sometimes writes about his annoyances with White People on his blog, on top of focusing on domestic abuse, queer, and sex positive topics. He is the editor of *Vagabonds: Anthology of the Mad Ones, Blood, Sweat and Fists*, and several other anthologies. A poet by blood and horror writer by heart, he is expecting his queer horror story collection *Carnage* to be released this fall. His latest book of poetry, *Cut the Loss*, was released July 2019. **https://degenerateweasel.weebly.com**

www.ingramcontent.com/pod-product-compliance
Lightning Source LLC
Chambersburg PA
CBHW050403030726
47503CB00006B/2004